THE CITY
IS
A WEB

by
JOHN WHITELEY

LONDON
PICKERING & INGLIS LTD
1976

PICKERING & INGLIS LTD
29 LUDGATE HILL, LONDON EC4M 7BP
26 BOTHWELL STREET, GLASGOW G2 6PA

ISBN 0 7208 2231 9
Cat. No. 11/3602

*Printed in Great Britain by Robert MacLehose & Co. Ltd,
Glasgow*

André's Ambition

1

"KINSHASA — CAPITAL OF THE Republic of Zaïre."

André Mokunzu repeated the words slowly to himself, in French. It sounded majestic to his ears when spoken slowly and solemnly in French. André felt he had to do something like this to seal the moment as something important. It was, after all, the fulfilment of all his dreams.

From his position on the boat, André could see precious little of the city, but his appetite was whetted, and every second brought him nearer.

The journey had been quick, coming downstream. The mighty Zaïre river, from which the country took its name, was a swift-flowing river, and favoured the downstream traffic.

"Admiring the city?" The voice came from behind him.

André spun round, and saw his cabin-mate standing there. André had shared his first-class cabin with a trader from Kinshasa, returning from a business trip.

"Yes," replied André. He turned back to look once more at the city. "It seems wonderful . . .

Look — there!"

A large, multi-storey building had just come into view. It was one thing to have heard of these buildings, and even to have seen pictures of them. Yet here they were looming up before him, reaching to the sky. It was an overwhelming experience. André gazed up in awe, wondering how these precariously-balanced giants did not topple over with the slightest gust of wind.

Now the boat was drawing near the busy river port where it would tie up. As it drew level with the port, the massive boat began to swing round. André noticed a couple of small tugs pulling at one end of the boat. He marvelled that such small boats could manoeuvre this large one with such ease.

In a few moments, the boat was sliding slowly and securely into position at the dockside. As he prepared to disembark, André's thoughts went back to the start of this great adventure.

*　*　*　*　*　*　*

"Father."

"Yes, my son?"

"I wish to speak to you," said André, diffidently.

"Then speak, my son. Have I ever refused to listen to you?" His father was mystified by André's reluctance, and a little annoyed.

"I am no longer a schoolboy, Father . . ."

"No, André," his father replied, his voice warming with pride. "It was a glad day for me to see my first son receive his diploma."

"My teacher said that I was one of the brightest boys in the class."

"He said this to you?" asked his father, with a penetrating look.

"No, Father. I — I heard him say it to you."

"Did you hear all he said?"

"Yes."

"And you want to talk to me about a journey?"

"Yes, Father. I heard him say that I could have a bright future."

"You wish to leave the village?"

"I have heard people speak of life in Kinshasa."

"So, that is it," his father sighed.

"They say that life is good in the city. I could get a job there. An office job. I would work every day in a suit and shirt. I would work all day at a desk. That is a good job, Father."

"Who has told you these things, André?"

"Many people."

"The other boys at school?" Again his father's look penetrated.

"Well, yes. But other people also."

"You know well that schoolboys have said many things which were not true."

"But Father, this really is true. Everybody says the same thing about Kinshasa."

"And have any of them been there?" asked his father, almost to himself.

"No, but . . ." André paused, unsure of himself.

"But I have heard our teacher speak of Kinshasa; and there are newspapers with photographs. Have you seen them, Father? The buildings are fine, and it is said they reach up to the sky, and . . ."

"Son," his father interrupted, "I have heard many other things about Kinshasa from the village elders. I have not heard the same things as you."

André was silent. One should not question what the village elders said — even if they were just uneducated old men who could only speak a word or two of French.

"Life is not easy there," his father continued. "Many people cannot find jobs, my son. They cannot grow their own food, for there is no land. They do not have enough to eat."

André was listening, but he did not want to hear.

"Are not these the things your teacher says?" asked his father, pausing for effect. "He is a missionary, and has been to Kinshasa many times. You know that he would only tell you the truth."

André knew what his father meant. He was to seek the advice of his teacher. He should not speak about it any more until he had done this.

The next day, André's father broached the subject.

"André, have you spoken to your teacher, yet?"

"Yes, Father," he replied unwillingly.

"What did he say?"

"He said that I should stay with you in the village, and perhaps help with the farming project."

"Yes, I know, my son. I have had it in mind for a long time. We have much work to do here for the Lord and for our people. We can start to teach the other people of the village better ways to grow food and to keep animals. We can . . ."

"No!" André broke in angrily. "All my education would be wasted. I want to work with my head, not my hands."

Indeed, for almost as long as his father had wanted André to do this, André had feared him asking it. It was the last thing he wanted.

His father sighed. How could his own son fail to realize that nothing he learned would be wasted? Already André read the Bible for his family, and for several others in the village who could not read for themselves. The pastor of the church had even asked if André could help with the reading classes.

His father's silence caused André to shuffle his feet uneasily. His sights were set on Kinshasa, and nothing less would do. He judged it better to bide his time, and wait until the opposition had died down — or was worn down.

One month, and many discussions later, the battle ended, quite unexpectedly.

His father was trying to bring another wearying talk to an end. "Son, do you realize how much it has cost us to educate you?"

André saw what he conceived to be his chance,

and seized it. "Yes, Father, and I don't want that money wasted. If I could go to Kinshasa, I could do something to gain advantage from my education."

"It is enough!" declared his father, with a despairing gesture of the hand. "I am getting old. This talk tires me. I will arrange for you to go. We will speak about it again tomorrow."

André had won at last. He found, however, that the taste of victory was not as sweet as he had expected. The whole thing made him feel wretched.

Next day, he went to his father to speak about the matter again.

"It is arranged," his father said. "We will write to Uncle Pierre. You will stay with him in Kinshasa. I have a little money which I had saved up for your future. You will need it — use it well . . ." He paused, as if undecided, or preoccupied. "Come, let us write the letter." Then he hurriedly dictated the letter to André.

When the letter was finished, he simply said, "Good, it is finished. We will send the letter tomorrow, and you can leave in a week's time. Prepare for your journey."

André realized how weary and burdened his father was feeling, by his unusual abruptness of speech. He tactfully retreated, leaving his father to his thoughts.

André's father said nothing more about the journey to his son, until the evening before he was due to leave.

"You realize, my son, that Uncle Pierre is not a Christian?"

"Yes, Father," said André, uneasily. He could guess what was coming.

"The pastor says there are many large churches in Kinshasa. The number of people who worship there is counted in hundreds, even in thousands. I hope you will find a good place to worship."

André was ill at ease when his father spoke about Christianity. Why did he always assume that his children would automatically accept his own beliefs? André had never quite known how to tell his father that he was educated, and wanted to think for himself. Nobody had ever encouraged him to talk about his doubts and questions, and he had developed a complex about them. They were things that could only be discussed clandestinely with the other boys at school.

Was now the time to tell his father all about it? He hesitated, and then decided against it. He was aware that his leaving had disturbed his father, and he did not want to hurt him any more. He tried to change the subject.

"Father, what if I should meet Simon in Kinshasa? The rumour is that he went there."

"I have told you André," his father replied sternly, "that we must forget that incident. We are Christians. God tells us that we must forgive others, just as He forgives us."

This was the sort of thing that André could not

take. He could see neither the need to be forgiven, nor the need to forgive other people who had done wrong.

"But he has stolen from us, Father. That is not easily forgotten."

"André, my son," cried his father in anguish, "why do you not find it in your heart to forgive? The police investigated the matter, and Simon was nowhere to be found. The time has come to forget."

"But what if I happen to meet Simon?"

"Once and for all, the matter is settled." His father's voice was trembling with emotion. "Surely you, my clever son, know that the people are counted in millions in Kinshasa. That means two thousand villages the size of ours, they tell me. You think to find him amongst all those people?"

André's father had never absolutely forbidden anything in this way before. He decided to apologize, so that his father would not remember him badly.

"I am sorry, Father. I will think no more of this."

He was pleased to see his father's approval, but unsure of his own ability to keep his promise.

The next day dawned, and André felt a slight twinge — his self-confidence wavered. If he was expecting a hero's farewell, he was let down. There was only the usual small group of people clustered round the transport lorry as it stopped in the village. However, the whole of André's family was gathered to bid him farewell.

Suddenly, the whole world seemed to collapse around him. His dream had come to an end even before it had started.

André's Arrival at Kinshasa

2   ANDRÉ'S FATHER FLUNG HIMSELF on his son, embracing him tightly, and André's mother had prostrated herself on the ground, clinging to his feet.

His father was whispering in his ear, "Don't go. Please don't go."

André needed an instant only to decide what to do. He had made too many plans to be stopped now, however much he coveted his father's approval.

"Father, Mother! Pull yourselves together!" he said in a grown-up voice. As soon as he said it, he doubted the wisdom of it. No young person ever spoke to their parents like this. He dreaded his father's reaction.

The reaction was entirely different from his fears.

"Yes, André. We have acted foolishly. It is bad to say such things when we have made all the arrangements for you to go. I am sorry, my son."

Then, seeing that almost the entire village was watching the small group, he addressed himself to André's mother. She was still weeping hysterically.

"Why does this always happen?" she wailed. "Why does education always take a mother's children from her?" Then she turned on her husband. "Why do you always send our children to school? It will always finish this way."

"Woman, be quiet," he said. "It is a shame for anyone to speak this way — especially a mother to her son."

In a moment, André's mother was calm. When his father decided everything was normal again, he said to his other children, "Come, it is time for us to say goodbye."

André's brothers and sisters took their turn at wishing him well, showing the appropriate emotions.

Then André's father gathered the family round him, and started to pray in a loud voice. André bowed his head, but kept furtively opening his eyes, wondering which of his friends would be laughing quietly to themselves. He found himself wishing that each sentence would be the last. This anxiousness made the prayer seem longer than it really was.

The prayer was fervent, like all the other prayers he had heard. On this occasion, it grew even more fervent as it progressed. Finally, the prayer became more broken, the rhythm became faster, and André's father broke into unashamed tears.

He threw his arms once again round his son's

neck.

"André, André, my son!" he cried. "You know I wish you well. Please make me proud to call you son. May you have success. May the Lord bless you. Write to us, won't you — every week? Your next brother will read your letters to us."

"Yes, Father. Have no fear. I will keep your face, and mother's, before me all the time," he said, referring to the photograph of his mother and father.

"Above all, André, keep your face turned towards Jesus. Never forget Him — even if you do forget us."

André smiled inwardly at his father's ability to turn almost anything into a religious exhortation. He hesitated, not knowing how to reply. Then he heard the noise of the lorry behind him.

"I must go, the lorry is starting," he said. He quickly turned, ran to the lorry, threw on his suitcase, then scrambled aboard himself as it started to move.

He waved to his parents and family, as they called to him, "Go well."

"Stay well," he called back.

He was still waving when a bend in the road took his family and village out of sight. He had been genuinely impressed by his father's display of obvious affection for himself, the oldest son. However, he was leaving the village and its way of life behind him and now he need not feel uncomfortable about his views on religion. Everybody in the city was educated. Of course, he mused, religion had its uses. It kept many people law-abiding — and that seemed to be the only hope for his great country now, after the bloodshed and rebellion that had scourged it. Deciding that these thoughts more or less summed up his beliefs, André settled down to the journey.

Seven days and four hours later, André stepped from the boat at the river port of Kinshasa. The port was teeming with passengers from the boat. He gripped his suitcase tightly and stepped out to find his fortune in the city.

The road outside the port was, if anything, even more chaotic than the port itself. Besides the passengers leaving the boat, there were passengers waiting to board, people coming to buy tickets, friends meeting people off the boat, and friends saying goodbye. The road was scattered with all manner of live animals, smoked fish, and other food.

Realizing that he did not know where to go, André asked someone if he knew the address of his uncle. That person was a stranger himself, so André decided to ask a taxi-driver. He had heard of taxis in the village, and the idea of being driven in a big car appealed to him. He chose the biggest and most impressive looking taxi, and walked over to it. He asked the taxi driver in his best French if he knew the address of his uncle, which he had written down.

The driver said nothing, but motioned André inside the car. He started the motor, and weaved his way through the crowds, cursing them as he went. He took André through many roads, and for a short way along a magnificent, wide boulevard. Then he plunged into a small side road, and it seemed to André as if they were back in the bush again. The road was rough, with no proper surface. The journey was through many such narrow, bumpy streets.

The journey went on and on, until André thought they must surely come out of the city, and drive out into the country again. When, after a little while, this did not happen, André changed his mind, and decided that they must be going round in circles. Perhaps the driver was showing him the city. Finally, they stopped.

"Here you are, son." It was the first time the taxi driver had spoken, and he spoke in Lingala.

André was taken aback at this, for he had expected everybody in Kinshasa to speak French. Lingala was the trade language used along the great river Zaïre, and known to most people in André's area. André had heard that much more patriotic feeling had been attached to Lingala of late, but this was the first time somebody had refused to reply to his French in French.

"Sixty makuta," demanded the taxi-driver, still in Lingala.

"How much?" asked André in surprise, and again in French.

"I said sixty makuta," said the driver, menacingly. "This is Kinshasa, not the bush." He seemed to be annoyed at André's French. The man was big, and his stubborn manner ruled out any discussion of the price.

André meekly paid up. Then he asked, "How did you know I am new to the city?" This time he was careful to use Lingala.

"Didn't I pick you up at the port?"

"Yes, but ..."

"It's easy to tell the new arrivals. Your clothes, your speech, your manner — everything about you. There are hundreds of new arrivals at the port every day."

"Please tell me," asked André, "did you give me a ride round the town before bringing me here?"

"Why should I waste time doing that?" the taxi-driver snorted. "I have a living to earn."

Still laughing to himself, he turned and got into the taxi, and sped off.

He left André wondering at the size of the city. When he had pulled himself together, André picked up his suitcase and turned to find his uncle's house. The address had given a number and the name of the road in which he was now standing. Seeing no numbers, he stopped a passer-by.

"Do you know where Tata Mokunzu lives,

please?" he asked.

"How should I know?" said the stranger, with a shrug of his shoulders, and walked on. André did not even have time to say 'Go well' to him. He was learning some of the different ways of the city people.

He went to the nearest house and spoke to the woman who was sitting over a wood fire outside the door.

"Greetings, Mama. Where does Tata Mokunzu live, please?" he asked, again in French.

She looked up blankly, indicating that she did not understand. André repeated the question in Lingala.

"He used to live there," she replied, pointing to the next house.

"Used to?"

"Yes, he has gone now."

"Where?"

"I don't know," she said resignedly, and turned back to her cooking pot.

"Thank you, Mama," said André, concerned at the news. "Stay well."

"Go well."

André turned, picked up his suitcase again, and made his way to the house indicated. He used Lingala again to tell the man sitting in the doorway that he was looking for his uncle, Pierre Mokunzu.

"He used to live here," said the man.

"Where does he live now?" asked André.

"But how should I know?" mumbled the man, astonished at the boy's stupidity in asking such a question.

"Where can I find him?" André asked, irritated at the manner of the city people.

Still the man did not answer.

"Can you not help me at all?" demanded André. He was becoming more infuriated.

Slowly the man rose to his feet, clucking with his tongue. "There are some people from his village in the next street."

He waved his hand in a vague indication of the direction. The gesture also announced that he was tired of talking to André, and that he considered the conversation closed.

Without another word, André picked up his suitcase again and turned away in disgust. His only clue as to where his uncle lived was a wave of a hand.

Suddenly, André felt very lonely.

André's Search Begins

3 WHEN ANDRÉ REACHED THE NEXT street, he started to walk along it, asking people questions. It did not matter what he asked — sometimes he asked for the direction to a shop or road, whose names he made up on the spur of the moment, or he asked people the time. He asked the questions in his tribal language, and in the dialect of his village.

After a dozen attempts, at each of which he had to repeat the question in Lingala, he was ready to give up. Just when he was thinking of moving to another street to try, a hand tapped him on the shoulder.

"Are you lost, boy?" a voice asked.

André spun round to see who had taken an interest in him. The face of the man was kindly, as if it was used to wearing a smile. Again André tried his tribal language.

"Where do you come from?" asked the man, replying in the tribal language.

"Mutondi, sir. I was told that some other people from my area live in this street. I am looking for my uncle, whose name is Mokunzu — Pierre

Mokunzu."

"Ah, yes," the man said. "Mokunzu. I know your uncle, or rather I knew him. I thought I recognized your face. I also lived in Mutondi, until I came to Kinshasa many years ago. How old are you now?"

"Nineteen."

"Yes, you would have been about eight or nine years old when I left the village. I saw you wandering about as if you were lost just now, and I thought I recognized you. So you are Pierre's nephew. Who is your father, and what is your name?"

"My father is called Alphonse, and I am André, sir," André replied, with great patience. "Can you tell me anything about my Uncle Pierre, please?"

"I can tell you some things, but they will not be good news for you, if you are looking for your uncle." The old man sighed, and continued, as if to himself, "I could tell you also what people say about your uncle, but it is not good to say those sort of things about people."

André's face fell as he realized that his chances of finding his uncle had rapidly returned to zero.

"Come to my house, and there we can talk of these things."

The old man took André into his house, and introduced him to his wife. She quickly got out their best chair, wiped the dust from it, and placed it for André to sit on.

The preliminaries over, the old man started talking in a low and serious voice.

"It was a thing of shame for us," he began. "Your uncle came, first of all, to live in a house in the next street."

"Yes," said André, "I went to that house, but they don't know where my uncle lives now."

"Nor does anyone, André. I must tell you this at the beginning. When your uncle came, he did not make friends with us, or with any of the people from the village. It seemed as if he was trying to break from the ways of our people."

André felt a little uncomfortable. He was also one who wanted to get away from the ways of his ancestors.

The old man broke off, and asked André, "Is your father a Christian?"

"Yes," replied André.

"I was not a Christian before I left Mutondi, but since we arrived here, both my wife and myself have become Christians." He paused, and seemed lost in his own thoughts again.

"Your uncle moved away from the house, and nobody knows where he lives now. He had a good job in a government office. Some say that he has a better job now. Some even say that he lives in a big European house, made with bricks, with many rooms, and big windows. . . . But this is just what people say. Nobody really knows."

"I am ashamed that I have not yet asked your

name," said André, when there was a lull in the conversation.

"My name is Ernest Mbokimwa." Another pause, then, "Your brother in Christ."

Another person, thought André, who thinks I am a Christian because my father is one. He was thinking of the best way to tell the old man that he was not a Christian, just because his father was one, when the man started talking again.

"Now," he went on, "we will do this. After you have rested, we will go to see the other people from our village to find out if they know anything about your uncle. However," and here he lapsed into the faraway voice, "I don't think we will be very successful."

"He must stay with us for as long as he is here — until he finds his uncle," interrupted the old man's wife.

"Yes, yes, of course." He hesitated before adding, "But we are very poor. There is no work here in the city, and life is very difficult. . . ."

His wife clucked her tongue, and grumbled, "It is shameful, this talk."

"Do not worry," said André. "I have some money, which I will have for my living expenses until I find a job. I will share some with you."

"André, this is a good thing you say. I feel shame, but I must accept your money." He paused, shook his head, and appeared to be about to say something, but stopped himself, and merely shook his head, saying, "Jobs, jobs."

"Do you have some paper, please? I would like to write to my father."

"I am sorry. We do not have any."

How poor could a person be, thought André, that he has not even any paper to write on? He did not voice his thoughts aloud, but politely asked where he could buy some paper.

The rest of the day was spent in composing the letter to his father. He started off with the bad news that he had not found his uncle. Then he spoke warmly of the man who had given him shelter, commending him to his father as a fellow Christian. André had to rewrite this part several times, so as not to give his father the impression that he considered himself a Christian also. Yet somehow it seemed too harsh to say, "The man who is looking after me also believes in your God." In the end, he had to leave his father with the wrong impression, for he could not find the right words to express exactly what he meant.

The letter finished, he was surprised to find that the nearest post office was over half an hour's walk away. By the time the letter was posted, André was tired. He returned to the house and fell fast asleep.

Next morning, the old man took André to see the other people from his village. None had any definite news. The only common factor in all the varied stories was that his uncle was supposed to have a job at the Ministry of Justice, and that he was supposed to live in a part of the city called Kalina. André noticed the special tone of voice in which some of the people said 'Kalina' and 'Ministry of Justice'. He asked about it afterwards.

"Kalina — that is a part of the city where many white people live. Some Zaïrians live there also — the very rich ones."

André's determination gained strength. If his uncle was a rich man, he was someone worth living with.

"As for the Ministry of Justice," continued the old man, "we respect law and justice. If he works for the government, he must be a great man."

André did not answer, but sighed inwardly. These people were still quite uneducated. Did they not understand that a government ministry could employ thousands of people, and that only the ones at the top were the really great men? Once again, André found himself feeling superior. However kind the man had been to him, clearly it would not do for André to go on living with him, especially once he had a job.

André formed his plan of action. He would go to the Ministry of Justice, and ask for his uncle. He would persist in his search. If he could not find his uncle at first, he would wander the streets of Kalina until he did. No pains would be spared. Whatever the hardship, he would find his Uncle Pierre.

He returned to the house, and collected a little money. Then he walked to the big road with much traffic, and hailed a taxi.

"Ministry of Justice!" he barked at the driver.

He sat back in the seat and tried to feel important. It felt wonderful to be driven everywhere he wanted to go, as long as he had money. André realized that the money he had now would not last him very long, but what did that matter when he would soon have a job, and earn much money?

The taxi took him along the same parts of the city by which he had come on the previous day. First, the seemingly endless streets of ordinary village-type houses with mud walls and tin roofs. Then they crossed the magnificent wide boulevard again, with the wonderful tall buildings. After that, there were streets full of splendid European houses.

How big they are, thought André. They must have at least five — no, six rooms in each house. It would be wonderful to live in a house like these.

Finally, the taxi drew up in front of a large building. It was not tall like some of the others he had admired so much, but it had something about it which appealed to him. It was wide and spacious. It was surrounded by colourful flower beds, and a lush green lawn. Truly, there never was grass like this before.

When André had paid the taxi-driver, and mounted the flight of steps, he looked back along the road which had brought him here. He was looking along a straight avenue, with long flower beds dividing the road in two. It was like a dream.

Still in his dream, he pushed open the door and entered the vast hall, marble-floored and gleaming. People were coming and going, and there seemed to be too many doors leading off this hall to count them all. Seeing a man seated at a desk near the entrance, André approached.

Having decided that French was the appropriate language to use here, he used his best French to ask, "Does a Mr Pierre Mokunzu work here, please?"

The man at the desk, who appeared to have been busy with something behind the desk, looked up, as if annoyed at the interruption. He looked André up and down with a scornful expression. He did not say anything, but seemed to be about to return to his more important task behind the desk, when two men came marching in and one of them rapped on the desk.

The man behind it was jerked back to attention, and asked them what he could do for them.

They demanded the whereabouts of a certain office, then strode off again as soon as the man had looked it up for them in a register he had on the desk.

When they had taken their leave, the man threw a glance at André which said, "Why are you still here?"

"Excuse me, can you tell me if . . ."

"Yes, I heard you first time," the man growled.

After waiting for an answer that did not come, André said, "Well, does he?"

"Does who? Does he what?" The man was irritated by André's continued presence there.

"Mr Pierre Mokunzu. Does he work here?"

"How should I know? There are thousands of people who work here. Should I know all their names?"

"But he's my uncle. I want to find him . . ." Even before he protested, André knew that it was hopeless.

"Are you going to leave, or do you want to be thrown out?" demanded the man, menacingly.

Dejected, André turned and slowly left the building. As he went, he looked at himself. He was scruffy, in his casual shirt, shabby trousers and old sandals. He was out of place in this building, where all the other people wore smart shirts, ties and suits.

He realized as he left the air-conditioned hall, and emerged into the heat of the day, that the dream was over. The clouds round his head dispersed, and his feet were once again truly on the ground.

In that moment, André realized that there was one thing which he had to do, before anything else.

Still Unsuccessful

4 BEFORE I CAN GET ANY FURTHER, André thought, I will have to buy myself clothes — smart clothes. I will need them anyway, when I get my job, and they may even help me find Uncle Pierre.

André sat down on the steps outside the building, and tried to recall his uncle. He was almost sure he would recognize him if he saw him again. André had been thirteen when Uncle Pierre had left the village, and the family had only had one letter from him since then.

The sun soon became hot, and André moved to a shady spot. He remembered his father's words to him before he left, that his uncle was not a Christian. For a moment it almost seemed as if that really mattered. The people in Kinshasa had found him unfriendly, and there were rumours about him back in the village. Some rumours said that he had been in trouble with the police, and that he was in prison; others said that he was a government minister, and even talked with the President of the Republic.

What did these rumours or his father's warning

matter? The only important thing about these rumours was that they bore some resemblance to what the people in Kinshasa thought, that his uncle worked in the Ministry of Justice. This was his only lead, and if it failed, André had nothing else to go on.

André sat by the entrance to the building all morning, watching the people coming and going, studying their faces carefully. Towards midday, when the sun was almost overhead, and shade was difficult to find, many other people came and waited, like him, near the doors.

Some had newspapers to sell, which they spread out in a display on the ground. Some women brought bowls full of food, which they also displayed on the ground. Others were ice cream sellers, on bicycles. Some just sat, like himself, with the same look of despair on their faces.

Soon, a friendly looking man came and sat by André, to share his precious square foot of shade.

"Why are all these people here?" André asked him.

"You are new to the city?" asked the man, and he went on without waiting on a reply, "Soon the people who work here will leave to go home. On Saturdays, they only work until noon." He paused, then added, "Are you looking for a job?"

"No," André replied, "I'm looking for my uncle." His mind, however, dwelt on the subject. He would have to find a job whether or not he found his uncle, and the thought of working here appealed to him, especially if it included only working in the morning on Saturdays.

Just then, people started pouring out of the building, and his companion went off in search of somebody. There were so many people that André only had the chance to look at a few, those nearest him. They went off in all directions, some stopping to buy things.

As suddenly as it had started, the hubbub and rush stopped, leaving only himself, and a few women putting their unsold food back in their bowls.

André walked away dejectedly. It began to dawn on him that he might have to make many such journeys before he found his uncle. In fact, if the truth were known, his confidence of ever finding his uncle was badly shaken.

This frame of mind made him more careful with his money, and he realized for the first time that he would not be able to take a taxi every time. Indeed, he might as well make a start at economizing now, and walk back to the house where he was staying.

He started out in the direction from which the taxi had brought him, and asked everybody whom he passed if he was going the right way.

It was a long journey, and his thoughts wandered as he walked. He thought of Simon. If he had so little chance of meeting his uncle, whom he had come to find, what chance would he have of ever coming across Simon? He had seen the warning light in his father's eyes when he had forbidden him to cause any trouble with Simon, but still his mind was full of the resentment he had first felt when they had discovered the theft.

His father had saved the money for his youngest brother to go to school. When Simon stole it, his brother had had to wait another year before he could start school. This was two years ago, but André was unable to forget, much less forgive.

It must have been this act of Simon's, André decided, that had led him to reject his father's religion. He felt hard when his father spoke of the need to forgive. His words had struck no answering chord within him. If people did wrong, they should be punished for it. André himself had seen that nobody was allowed to forget the matter of Simon, by bringing it up before he left.

His thoughts also wandered to Ernest Mbokimwa, and his heart softened. He was secure in the knowledge that the old man had taken André to his heart as warmly as he had taken him into his home. He knew that he was sure of a shelter as long as he needed it. André was determined not to abuse this kindness.

The journey was long, and seemed longer than any journey he had made previously. He had certainly walked as far as this before, but in the village he would have had to walk through many shady jungle paths to walk a distance as long as this. Here in the city, he could only walk along streets with little shade.

He arrived at his temporary home three hours after he started walking. Ernest was pleased to see him back, and eagerly asked how he had got on.

"Not very well, Tata. I have walked a long way, and I am thirsty. May I have a drink? Then I will tell you the story."

"Please, you may call me Ernest," the old man replied, as he poured a glass of water from the tap. "Remember you are my brother in Christ."

André shifted uneasily in his chair. He would feel ashamed at calling a person as old as his father by his Christian name. The fact that the old man had suggested it because he believed André to be a Christian made him doubly uncomfortable. He longed to explain that he was not a Christian just because his father was. He tried to search for the right way of saying it, and again he could not find the right words. However he thought of it, it seemed as if he would be deceiving this man who had showed him kindness.

"May I just call you Uncle?" he suggested. "You are so much older than I am."

"Yes, if you feel happier. Now, André, you are discovering how big this city is?"

"Yes," replied André, "I don't know how far I have walked, but at home, I would have had to walk out into the forest, past Nganzie, and even past Lubuku, to have walked the same distance.

33

But here, there were streets and houses all the way — without a break."

Ernest nodded at the mention of the two neighbouring villages. He carried on nodding or shaking his head as André told him all that had happened that day. When André finished, he sighed.

"So you are discovering some of the difficulties of living in the capital. People are hard. They are rude and impatient. In fact we all become rude and impatient and hard here," and, brushing away André's protest with his hand, he added, "It is very hard to be a good Christian here."

André tried to change the subject. "Life is good in some ways, though."

"Many people are beginning to realize that life was better back in the village. I have no education, and I cannot find work easily. Sometimes I cut grass; sometimes I chop wood — I do anything I can to earn money."

"I have a certificate of education . . ." André started.

"And you want to get a job writing at a desk. That's what they all want, but not many of them find jobs."

"Do not worry, I will get a job." André was confident of his ability. "First, I will buy a suit, a white shirt, and a smart pair of shoes. I will need them for the job, and they may help me find my Uncle Pierre."

The older man wore a tired look on his face, reminding André of his father's face before he left. It was a face which said, "Go ahead, young man. You must discover these things for yourself. How many times have I tried to convince people of this sort of thing. But now I see that people will not be convinced of anything until they discover it for themselves. I have to stand by and let them find out."

After André had eaten with Ernest and his family, he felt tired, and excused himself.

"You wish to go to church with us tomorrow?" asked Ernest, although it was not really a question.

The prospect of these big churches appealed to André, and he readily agreed. Although he had doubts about his father's religion, he still enjoyed going to church.

He awoke early next morning, and made himself as smart as he could, to accompany Ernest and his family to church.

André enjoyed his first service in Kinshasa. He had always enjoyed singing, and loved to hear a church full of people singing at the tops of their voices. He was enchanted by the men's choir, and the women's choir, and the youth choir, and the brass band accompanying the hymns.

When the pastor asked all newcomers to stand up so that they might be welcomed, he stood erect, as if to impress those present that people from Mutondi were something special.

When the collection basket came round, he only put in a small coin thinking that it might be a long time before he could find a job.

Too soon the taking of the collection was over, and André had to listen to the sermon. This was the part of the service he liked least, and as it always came last, he considered the service was really finished before the sermon. He found himself trying to find fault with what the preacher said. It had become so much of a habit in his own village church that now he did it without thinking.

André Finds His Uncle

5 NEXT DAY, ANDRÉ SET ABOUT getting a fine suit of clothes. He went to the tailors, and was measured. Then he went to buy a white shirt, and a tie, and a pair of socks. Finally, he bought a pair of shoes.

This apparently simple process took nearly the whole day, for André wanted to appear like one of the Kinshasa people. This consisted of examining every item in each shop, pretending to look at them carefully, and rejecting them for some obscure reason. He did this in most shops without buying anything, until he tired of it, or could not find any other shops selling what he wanted. When he actually made his purchases, he chose something at random.

At the end of the day, hoping he had made a good impression, he went back to the tailor, where his suit was cut out and pinned together. He tried it for size, and the tailor made a few adjustments.

The next morning, André was at the tailors as soon as it opened, which meant that he had to wait for an hour while his suit was finished. When it was ready, he tried it for size, paid for it, and hurried back to Uncle Ernest.

He changed into his new clothes, and realized that almost all of his father's money had gone on these clothes. The occasion seemed to call for something special, so André took a little of the money that was left, and went to find a taxi.

The taxi drew up at the Palais de Justice. André quickly paid the taxi-driver, and got out, trying to look important. He strode confidently up the steps of the building, in through the glass doors, and made straight for the reception desk. He adjusted his tie as he walked. Arriving at the desk, he rapped on it sharply.

The man behind the desk looked startled as André said abruptly, "Mr Pierre Mokunzu — which office?"

The man replied equally abruptly, "Why do you want to see him?"

André was not sure how he should react, and tried to be bold. "Don't speak to me like that. It is a very urgent matter." He paused for a fraction of a second. "A matter of life and death." He did not like telling lies, and wondered whether he was convincing.

"Who are you?"

Again André hesitated, wondering whether to claim to be his son. "I am his nephew. I must see him. Please tell me where he is."

"I don't think there is anyone of that name works here," said the man, slowly, scratching his head. André had the uncomfortable impression that the man had seen through his pretence and was laughing up his sleeve.

"Nonsense, I know he works here." The act was becoming more difficult.

The man said nothing, but took out a book from a drawer and placed it before André.

André, at a loss for words, looked enquiringly at the man.

"That is a list of employees and the offices where they work. I tell you that Pierre Mokunzu does not work here. Do you want to check?"

He sounded so confident that André almost gave up. Just to keep up his part, he looked through the book, certain however that he would not find his uncle's name there. His eyes scanned the pages carelessly. Suddenly, as he was running down a column of names, he stopped. He looked again. He had not looked at the crossed out names properly before, but there it was. Pierre Mokunzu — Bureau 27.

His confidence returned, and he said, triumphantly, "There," pointing to his uncle's name.

"That's what I said. His name is crossed out, which means that he doesn't work here any more."

André was at once glad and sorry — glad that he had a definite lead, but sorry that it did not take him very far. His voice returned to normal. "When did he leave?"

The man at the desk had turned away, and was

not even listening any more.

Just then, someone tapped André on the arm.

"Did I hear you mention Pierre Mokunzu?" asked a large man.

"Yes, I'm looking for him," said André, eagerly.

"I expect you're another one after money, eh? Getting to be a habit now, all these people coming looking for him. He must have been a scoundrel."

"Do you know where he lives or works now?" asked André, disregarding the man's accusations against his uncle.

"Well, I heard that he forged a signature and got a job at the Post Office."

"Thank you," said André, and turned away despondently. The only thing he could do was to look for his uncle at the Post Office. But which Post Office? There was one in each commune. He decided to go first to the Central Post Office.

Next day, again dressed in his best clothes, André found the Central Post Office. At least, he thought, he would have no difficulty in hanging around here all day if he had to. There were seemingly hundreds of people doing just that already, and many more coming and going as if they had something to do.

He went into the large building and looked round the great hall. All around the walls were counters, with people clustered round them, and windows behind which the Post Office clerks sat. André walked slowly round until he saw a window marked 'information'. There were not many people around this window, so he managed to remain reasonably dignified.

"Excuse me," he asked, as politely as he knew how, "I am looking for Mr Pierre Mokunzu. Does he work here?"

"He doesn't work here," said the man, waving his hand into the office behind him. "He might work in another department."

"Don't you have a list of all the people who work here?"

"Sorry. You can try all the departments. There are administration, philately and radio licences upstairs, the savings accounts down that corridor, the sorting office on this side of the corridor, the telegraph department over the other side of the hall, and all the offices which open to the hall, of course. Then downstairs there is the parcels office . . ."

"Oh, I see," said André, a little overwhelmed.

"You would need to go to each of the departments and ask there."

"Thank you for being so helpful," replied André, as he walked slowly away. He decided to start with all the departments on the same level as he was now. Several hours later, having exhausted all the possibilities, as far as he could see, on that floor, his determination had not wavered, and he decided to try downstairs at the parcels office.

To get downstairs, he had to go out of the

building, and then go round to the parcels department at the side of the building. He was just turning the corner, when in his hurry he bumped into someone.

Looking up to apologize, he was suddenly paralysed into inaction.

"André!" the man exclaimed.

"Uncle Pierre!" said André.

A look of annoyance crept into his uncle's face, but it was immediately overcome by a smile. It was a weak smile, as if he were embarrassed at meeting André.

"Uncle, I have been looking everywhere for you. I have been in the city five days now. We wrote to you at your old address, not knowing that you had moved away."

"Well, so you have come to visit me in the city?"

"Yes, I have come to find work. A friend of father's has been looking after me until I found you."

"But we haven't got a big house, there is no room for you to stay."

"But Uncle, you can't turn me out, not one of the family."

His uncle hesitated, then said, "It wouldn't be turning you out. You could stay with these other friends, and I will help you find work." He took a piece of paper from his pocket, and began writing. "Here is my address, come and see me this evening, after work."

With that, he strode off, looking important again in his smart suit.

André was left holding the piece of paper, and feeling even more depressed than he had been during all the time he had been looking for his uncle. The welcome had been less than enthusiastic. André went back to his Uncle Ernest's small house, and told him what had happened, but not saying that his Uncle Pierre had come very near to refusing to take him in. To André's mind this was incomprehensible. People just did not refuse hospitality to other members of their family.

"I shall be sorry to leave you, but I know how difficult it has been for you to have me here. I cannot say how grateful I am to you. At the moment, I feel that you are more of an uncle to me than he is."

"You are welcome to stay here if you wish."

"No, Uncle Ernest. I promised myself that I would not abuse your kindness, and my uncle can afford to look after me better than you can. Besides, he has a duty to the family."

"Please, then, at least come and visit us. We will see you at church, of course?"

"Yes, I will come, and I will never forget your kindness to me. Now, I must get things ready to leave."

In an hour, all André's possessions were packed, and he was ready to leave, but with a heavy heart. He showed the address his uncle had given him to

Uncle Ernest.

"Where is this, Uncle?"

"I think it is in Kalina somewhere. I have never been there."

"Thank you. I will find it," said André.

So André set off on foot for his uncle's house. He had with him all his possessions, now augmented by a fine suit of clothes, what was left of his father's money, and more than his fair share of optimism about finding a job. He wondered how his Uncle Pierre would receive him.

A Great Disappointment

6 IT WAS EVENING WHEN ANDRÉ arrived at his uncle's door. Nervously, he knocked and Uncle Pierre answered it.

"André," he said enthusiastically. Then when he saw what André had brought with him, his face changed. "But you've brought everything with you. I told you we couldn't have you here."

André swallowed hard, and said, "The people I was with said I had to leave. I had no choice." This was the second time he had deliberately told a lie, and it was still an effort, although he found it a little easier this time. He attempted to justify himself by imagining that special circumstances required special measures.

"Well, I told you we haven't enough room," insisted his uncle.

André felt a wave of indignation. "But this is a big house. That room," he added, pointing over his uncle's shoulder into the house, "is bigger than the whole house I was staying in. Besides, what do you think would happen if I wrote home and told them that you had refused to take me in when I had nowhere else to go?"

Suddenly, his uncle's face changed. He did not speak for a moment. André could see that he was thinking deeply; weighing up the pros and cons, trying to find a way round. At that moment, by the sort of intuition that is supposed to be the prerogative of women, André knew his uncle. He knew him to be a calculating, contriving man. A man whose ways would always be devious. He was ready to believe the stories of his uncle's dishonesty.

"Come in," said his uncle at last, then added, in a guarded sort of way, "we will see what we can do for you."

André could feel the unfriendly atmosphere as he walked in. He was introduced to his Aunt Hélène, and to his cousins, in a stiff, formal manner.

It seemed to André as if his uncle was conveying a message of caution to his family by his manner. "This is an intruder," it said, "we must not become unduly friendly with him, and on no account make him feel at home."

André did not like his Aunt Hélène. She was neither African in her dress, nor European. Even in her language she was changeable. Sometimes she spoke in French, and sometimes in Lingala. He never heard her speak in the tribal language.

Try as he would, André could not find one thing in this house or family which he liked. It would certainly be unpleasant living here. The realization came to André that perhaps this was his uncle's way of trying to get rid of him. Just make things so unpleasant that André would leave of his own accord.

Well, thought André, if that is how they are trying to do it, they won't succeed. I will stick here no matter how bad it gets. In fact, I can even make it unpleasant for them.

His uncle questioned him closely about his prospects of a job. André in his turn tried to sound as optimistic as he could, with little justification but his own optimism.

Next day, André found his way to the Ministry of Justice, looking as smart as he could make himself. Armed with his certificate of education, he found his way to the door marked 'Personnel Officer', where he was told to wait. He sat on a chair in the corridor and waited. Two hours passed before anybody took any notice of him.

A man who was passing asked him what he wanted, and when he was told, passed on apparently unconcerned. A short while later a woman appeared at the door and beckoned him in. He was ushered to a seat in front of a desk.

The desk was large, and an important looking man glowered at him from the other side of the desk. The man was short and fat, and had the air of a bad tempered dog.

"You want a job?" he barked.

"Yes, sir."

"Education?"

André had his certificate ready, and handed it over the desk. He found this operation difficult, for the desk was so large that he had to get up from his seat to reach over. Yet, somehow, it seemed inappropriate to move from the chair, lest the big dog should bite him.

The man looked over the certificate slowly, his lips moving silently as he read it to himself. Suddenly his face changed. He looked up at the ceiling, muttering André's name.

"Mokunzu, Mokunzu." He awoke from his dream, and snapped an order at his secretary, the woman who had opened the door for André. "Mokunzu — file."

She dutifully searched and produced the file from the murky depths of a steel cabinet.

"Ah, yes," said the personnel officer, with apparent satisfaction. He pointed an accusing finger at André. "Are you related to Pierre Mokunzu?"

André wilted before the question. "Yes, sir, he is my uncle."

"Then the matter is finished. I am sorry, but we have no job for you here."

André sat there stupefied, while the man turned away and occupied himself with something else. The man looked up after a few moments, and seemed surprised to see André still there. He called his secretary to show André out.

Completely demoralized, André slowly picked up his certificate and went. He had no need to ask why he had been treated in this way. He knew that all his suspicions about his uncle were true.

On arriving back at his uncle's house, he told his aunt that he had not been successful. She showed no sympathy.

"Did nobody tell you that jobs are not easy to get here? Why don't you go home?" she suggested, trying unsuccessfully to disguise her anxiety to get rid of him as concern for his well-being.

André felt no comfort, for he could see through her sham. All she and her husband wanted was to get him out of the house. He even thought that they would probably have been willing to give him the money for his fare home if they could get rid of him that way.

* * * * * * *

During the next six months, this scene was repeated many times. André tried to find work in every conceivable place, following up many suggestions of his uncle's, and finding out many for himself.

None of his attempts produced a job. Sometimes he was refused straight away; sometimes he had to be interviewed. Sometimes he was asked for bribes, which he would gladly have paid if he had had any money.

Every time he returned with his story of

disappointment his uncle became more and more angry. Finally, he accused André of laziness and threatened to throw him out.

During this time, André had become hardened to life in the city. He became one of the thousands of jobless who roamed its streets and only existed by virtue of the ancient custom of their people which required members of a family to care for each other. André was more fortunate than most — he lived with a fairly wealthy family.

He continued going to the big church for the first weeks. He met his 'Uncle' Ernest there, and was happy in the company of friends for at least a few hours each week. Then, because the distance was so great, he missed one or two weeks.

When he did not go to the big church in the city, he went to a nearby church which had services in French. Soon the routine had changed to regular visits to the French speaking church, and only occasional visits to the big church in the city.

The French speaking service held a certain appeal for André. Besides the important looking Zaïrian citizens who went there, there were many Europeans. Somehow, André felt, he had found his niche there.

Living with Uncle Pierre had its effect on him. Even though he was an unwelcome guest, he found himself picking up their ways, and some of their language. In these surroundings, he found it gradually easier to produce the half-truths and white lies that he thought would help him get a job.

At the end of six months, he felt more at ease in his uncle's house even though he did not feel any more welcome than when he first arrived. He had become more like them.

By the end of six months, the novelty of going to the French speaking service had worn off, and he had not been to the big church in the city for months. Even then, he had felt uncomfortable, and for some unaccountable reason, he had deliberately avoided Ernest, and hurried back to his uncle's house as soon as the service had finished. He felt instinctively that he would never go there again.

André had not found new objections to his father's faith, as he had tried to do before. He was living in an atmosphere where these beliefs were not talked about. It was not long before he stopped thinking about them. Once he had tried to combat them; now it just did not seem important any more.

All that was important was the grim reality of living in the hostile city. Here, everything had to be fought for, and everybody was a potential enemy, because they either had or were looking for a job which could have been his. His father's religion was not relevant to this sort of existence.

André wrote less and less to his father. On the few occasions that he had written, he always told his father that he really was sure the next interview would produce a job.

André received regular fortnightly letters which his father dictated. Always, they demanded more information. His father wanted to know more about the church André attended, more news of his brother Pierre, more about what life was really like in the city.

All these requests André ignored. He knew that if he answered them, he would show himself in a bad light, even if this was the true light. He would have had to admit that he had been a failure, and he did not want to admit that to himself, let alone to his father.

André had also used this time to try to find Simon. He did not really know what he would do if he ever found him, but a vague, senseless desire for revenge burned within him. He started his search by taking a day off from his search for a job, and tried to find out where Simon might live. He soon discovered that some people from Nganzie, Simon's village, lived not far from his first home in Kinshasa.

Yes, the people from Nganzie had seen Simon. He had lived in this very road, once. Now he had gone, and nobody knew where he was. André went to see the man with whom Simon had lived. His first question was if he knew where Simon lived now.

"Nobody knows. He left one night while we were all asleep. In the morning there was no trace of him. He had taken all his things and left." The man's voice had risen and gained in emotion as he spoke. He went on, "If you find him, I want to know where he is."

André hesitated before asking the next, delicate question. "Are you his brother?"

"Yes."

"Same mother, same father?"

"No, we are not close relatives."

André's face fell, for he knew that although this man called Simon his brother, he was only a distant relative. He had hoped to be able to press him for the stolen money.

The man saw André's expression, and asked, "Does he owe you money also?"

"Er, yes," replied André, confused.

"That makes four people who have come to me with the same story since he left!" the man shouted, displaying the said number of fingers in front of André's face. "I will not be responsible for his debts, do you hear? He also owes me money, and I will never see that again."

André tried to get more information as to where he might find Simon, or as to where Simon had been before he left. The man could tell him nothing, however. André left with weary steps.

Since that time, André had asked about Simon everywhere he went on the chance that someone might have seen or known him. So far, he had had no success.

As the weeks and months followed each other in

dreary procession, his optimism died a slow, tormenting death. His hopes of finding a job faded, and he tried to replace them with hopes of finding Simon. The search for Simon began to take on as much importance as the search for a job had done.

Now, six months after he had arrived in the city, he had only one hope. He must get away from this city which turned its unwelcoming back upon visitors. He must get away from his Uncle Pierre with his city manners. Uncle Pierre and his family who had made André so like themselves — dishonest, hard, unfriendly.

André saw one way of achieving this. He would sell his suit, upon which he had placed such fond hopes once, and buy his ticket to return home on the river boat. He would have to swallow his pride, and ask his father to take him back. It would probably be welcome news for his uncle when he decided to tell him.

André little realized the turn events would take, and how they would relieve him of the necessity of telling his uncle of his plans.

André Leaves His Uncle

7 ANDRÉ HAD FORMULATED HIS PLAN
to return home, and was on the point of telling his
uncle when it happened. His uncle started
questioning him again on what he was doing about
getting a job, and André was finding it more and
more difficult to keep his uncle satisfied with his
answers. He became irritated.

His uncle also became irritated, and it took only
a few moments for a blazing quarrel to erupt. They
both became angry and shouted at each other.
André felt that the sooner he left this house the
better. He awaited his opportunity.

"If you keep on this way," his uncle raged, "I
shall have to put you out!"

"There's nothing I should like better!" shouted
André, his face quivering with fury. All the faces in
the room were turned towards him. He continued,
"In fact, I am ready to leave right now. This will
be the happiest day since I came here."

His uncle's eyes narrowed, and he spoke in a low
voice, white-hot with emotion. "The sooner the
better," he said, and stalked off to André's room.

André followed him, in time to see his uncle

throwing all his possessions out of the window. Without another word, André retrieved his suit, now more precious to him than ever before, and left the house.

He picked up what possessions he could find outside the window, and walked away in no particular direction. The only thing he could think of was to put as much distance as possible between himself and that house.

André slept that night in a doorway of a large building, the best shelter he could find. He was woken up early in the morning by somebody prodding him with a stick. He raised his stiff body to a vertical position, and looked around. The man who had woken him told him to go away before the police came and arrested him.

He found his way to the river port, and waited until it opened. He wanted to discover the fare, so that he would know how much money he would need to get from the sale of his suit.

When he was told the price, he gave a low whistle. "That's nearly double the price of the fare I paid to come here!"

"When did you come?" asked the clerk.

"Six months ago."

"The fares have gone up since then. Besides, don't forget that the upstream fare is more than the downstream fare, because the trip takes longer."

André had not thought of that. He paused, thinking, and then inquired the price of a second or third class ticket.

He found his way into the town, and made straight for the place where he knew he could sell his suit. He walked into the dark shop, making his way through the second-hand suits hanging from the low ceiling.

The shopkeeper looked at the suit, pretending he was not really interested in it. André was very good at bargaining and managed to get what he considered to be a fair price. He had enough for a second class ticket and the fare for a ride on the lorry, and a little left over to buy some food until the boat left in a few days' time.

He walked out of the shop, clutching the bundle of notes on which all his hopes were pinned. He went straight back to the river port to buy his ticket.

Thinking about it afterwards, André could not quite remember what had happened. The port was crowded with people coming and going, jostling one another in confusion. Then André thought he heard the noise of a couple of men in violent argument. He stopped, turned and looked in that direction. At the same moment, he seemed to have been jostled by someone going in the opposite direction.

When the fuss had all died down, André turned and went on to the ticket office. It was then he realized that his money had gone.

As a safety measure, he had put it in his pocket

before reaching the port. Now it was gone. In a panic, he searched in all his other pockets in case he had made a mistake. He had made no mistake, his money was gone.

At the disappearance of his only hope, desperation overtook him. André sat down and wept openly and bitterly, but there was nobody to comfort him. After a few minutes, he regained control, and went to tell his story to the port police. There were a couple of them standing by the huge gates at the entrance. He half expected the reply he got.

"What do you expect me to do about it?" said the policeman. "The only thing you can do is to report the loss to the police in the city. If you can tell them who stole your money, then they will arrest him."

André walked slowly away from the port. He knew that he should report the loss to the police, but he also knew he would never go there. He spent the rest of the day wandering about aimlessly, his mind too full of the tragedy that had overtaken him to do anything.

He spent the night sleeping under a tree in a small open space he found.

Next day, awakening at dawn, he got up and stretched his stiff arms and legs. When he had recovered his senses he remembered his plight. At least the sleep had given him some relief from worrying about it. He walked along a little way, and then sat down to think hard.

All that mattered was getting home. The root of the problem was that without money he could not possibly get home. How could he get enough money and be sure of not getting it stolen? Suddenly, he had an idea. The missionaries!

The church in his village had been started by missionaries long ago. They had a Zaïrian pastor now, and no missionaries lived there any more. The church, however, was still connected to the mission, and missionaries occasionally visited the village. There was also André's old schoolteacher.

André could never decide on the status of his old teacher. He was a European, and apparently a member of the missionary society. The difference was that he was a teacher, and lived by himself in the village. The other missionaries who occasionally visited the village were pastors.

Now, André knew that the headquarters of the mission were in Kinshasa somewhere. If only he could find them, they surely would help him when they found out what had happened. They would understand, especially if he laid it on thick about being repentant, and wanting to go back to the village to help his father who was a loyal church member . . .

* * * * * * *

. . . It had been a tiring morning for George Andrews. The frustration had started mounting when he had had to wait for over an hour to see a government official.

When he was finally ushered into an office, he had burst out angrily, "I am the legal representative of our mission, and my appointment was for an hour and a half ago."

"I am sorry, but the person who deals with your society had to leave on urgent business," he was told.

"It's about the subsidies for the new hospital," he had said.

"Yes, well, I'm afraid I can only take your papers and give them to him when he comes in. Perhaps you can make an appointment for to-morrow, or shall I ask him to ring you?"

After the hour and a half wait, it had all been over in less than five minutes. He stalked out.

Then when he was leaving, the car would not start. He had to ask two people to push with him, and they had angrily demanded a tip for doing it.

Back at his own office, he looked through the morning mail, which depressed him even more.

George went home for his dinner, and unloaded all his troubles on his wife.

"I've had a terrible morning, dear. First of all I tried to get something moving on those hospital subsidies, then the car wouldn't start, right in the middle of town. Then there were letters from young Bill Gardner, and Mary Crompton."

"Oh, and are they managing to get their problems

sorted out?"

"Of course not! What do you expect with those two? These new missionaries nowadays think they know everything after they've been here a couple of years, and want everything run their own way. What was it we were told? During our first three years we should keep our eyes open and our mouths shut."

"Do you feel better now you've got that off your chest?" asked his wife, smiling. "You've been working too hard lately. Why not ease up? You won't do yourself or your work any good by over-working — even if it is God's work."

"Yes, that's right of course, my dear," he said, and now he was smiling, too. "You always bring me back . . ."

His words were interrupted by a knock at the front door, and the smile left his face. He got up and strode out to see who it was.

"That was quick, dear," said his wife, as he returned. "Who was it?"

"Some young fellow with a hard luck story. Said he came from Mutondi. He didn't forget to say that his father was a member of our church there. He claimed he had been in the city for months trying to find work, and was trying to get home when someone stole all his money."

"Oh, the poor lad."

"Personally, it's the ones with the longest stories that I'm least inclined to believe. Anyway, I told him that we couldn't help him. There wasn't any part of his story he could prove."

"Oh, dear, that's a hard thing to do," commented his wife, "but I suppose he will have some friends or relations to help him."

"He had some story about a wicked uncle who refused to help him, and threw him out."

"Well, if that's true, it's a terrible situation to be in."

"Don't make me feel too guilty about it, dear. I feel bad enough already."

"I know, dear, sorry. If only we could offer them something."

"He asked if we had any work he could do to earn some money."

"At least he was willing to do that."

"I just couldn't say yes, though. We took on that old fellow from the church in the city last week. There really isn't enough work for him, but it helps him out of a tough spot. Our resources are being stretched to the limit as it is."

André is Caught

8 ANDRÉ TRUDGED WEARILY through the streets, with a chip on his shoulder. Nobody was interested in him, and he had decided that he would never take any thought for anybody again. He had always known that missionaries were hypocrites, and his recent unpleasant experience only confirmed this.

He wandered around aimlessly, seeking only a hospitable corner in which to spend the night. For the moment he could only scratch a living by any means available — fair means or foul. After that — well, the future would have to look after itself.

His brain was weary — too weary to exercise itself on any more plans to get home. He was not even sure any more that he wanted to go home. All that mattered now was the grim business of existing from one day to another, and finding a place to lay his head each night.

From that time, he lived the life of a beggar. When he could not beg money, he tried to get a little money by doing menial things for white people. He would offer to look after their cars while they went into the shops, or offer to carry their bags for them when they came out. For these services, he was given a small tip, sometimes almost thrown at him. He noticed also an occurrence that happened too often to be a coincidence. Sometimes the people would "accidentally" drop the coin as they were giving it to him, and he would have to pick it up from the ground. He had heard that such people existed — Europeans who did not like to touch Africans, even to shake hands. The experience of meeting them was not pleasant.

It was not long before André took a big step — one which proved to be decisive.

He was guarding the car of a white person, and brooding on his ill fortune, and the way people ill-treated him. The white man came out of the shop, with another person carrying his bags full of shopping.

"He looks like one of those sort," thought André, expecting to have to bend down for his money. "I've a good mind to refuse it if he does. Oh, if only I didn't need the money."

Just then, he noticed that the white man had dropped his wallet. He was searching in his pocket for a small coin to give André, and had not noticed it. With a slight shift of his position, and a barely perceptible movement of his foot, André managed to put his foot over the wallet to hide it. The man got into the car and drove off quickly.

André's hand trembled as he bent down to pick up the wallet. He had looked round to see that nobody was watching, and tried to appear as un-concerned as he could. His hand reached down underneath his foot. Then it was actually holding the wallet.

He looked in the wallet. There was a wad of notes, more than enough to get him home! His heart skipped a beat, and he felt a moment of elation. The moment was short-lived. His heart dropped as he felt a heavy hand on his shoulder.

In the split second that followed, he wondered if he would stand any chance if he tried to run, rejected the possibility and tried to form the outline of a story that he had just noticed the wallet and was looking to see if there was any name and address in it.

When he turned round, he saw that the hand on his shoulder was not the long arm of the law. The first surprise that it was not a policeman flitted across his face. Then he put on an indignant voice.

"What do you want?" he snapped.

The man who was holding him was young, and dressed quite smartly. He spoke excellent French.

"Why are you so jumpy?" he said, simply. "Do you feel guilty about something? Come, now, I am a friend."

The words oozed out of his mouth like syrup. His voice was soft, but the grip on André's arm was iron hard.

In a flash André took in the situation. The man's pointed question indicated clearly that he had seen what had happened. At the same time André detected something fishy about him. His hair, which had suffered from a half-hearted attempt at straightening; his clothes, that bit too smart and colourful; his voice; his attitude; all spoke eloquently of something artificial. André was temporarily silenced, and groped around the recesses of his mind for the best way to answer him. The man continued speaking.

"Yes, my friend, you were seen," he said.

"But . . ." André tried to object.

"But you did not see me?" The man seemed able to read his mind. "Let us say that nobody ever sees me unless I wish it." A smile spread across his face, a smile as sickly as his voice. He seemed pleased with himself, and seemed to be enjoying the way he had expressed himself.

"Come with me," he said, and suddenly he moved, half dragging André with him. André tried to resist, but the pressure on his arm was too much.

The man took André to a big car with slightly darkened windows. André realized how he had been spotted. The man pushed André into a front seat. Then, with a lightning movement, he took the wallet from André's dazed grasp, and put it in the glove compartment, locking it afterwards.

"I think it is better if I take possession of that."

"What are you going to do?" asked André, desperately. "Take me to the police?"

"Let us say that that would be the last resort. If

you force me to do it, then I will hand you over."

What was this he was saying? How would André force him to take him to the police station? Surely it should have been the other way round?

"You see, young man, I want to help you. I believe that people like you should be given a chance." Again the pause for effect.

"Well?" said André, trying to understand the situation.

The man did not answer, but started the car, and drove a little way before he spoke.

"I like you, young man."

"Uh?" André voiced his bewilderment.

"I liked the way you moved just then. It was a very clever operation, purely from the professional point of view, of course."

The light dawned. André realized what was fishy about this man, and rather naïvely, he voiced his thoughts.

"You're a crook?"

"Come, come. That's an ugly word. You know that riches are a burden to people. I merely relieve them of their burdens whenever I can, with the help of some colleagues." He laughed heartily at his joke.

André did not laugh. Finding himself in the power of a crook, and a gang leader, if he could believe that last comment, was not a laughing matter.

"Now," said the man, "we have been on the

look-out for a long time for a young man like yourself. Someone with your aptitude, and your abilities. We can offer you a good living, and a roof over your head, and the means to enjoy life a little. What is life if we cannot enjoy it?"

No, thought André, this is worse than anything. He seems to be offering me a place in his gang, or he will turn me over to the law. In fact, there seemed to be no choice at all. The only thing that brightened the outlook was that if what the man said was true, there was at least some hope of getting enough money for perhaps the return home, and an end to this life of begging. Hope flared momentarily inside André, lighting up the future — the path leading home.

André's thoughts were interrupted as the other man swore at another driver.

The journey was soon over, and they got out of the car together in the driveway of a big house which they entered. Some other young men were in one of the rooms discussing something loudly and laughing. They stopped when they heard the noise of the door, and came to see who it was.

"Hello, boss," said one of them.

"Who's he?" sneered another, pointing at André.

"Now, boys, I want you to meet our new member. He's just the person we've been looking for. What did you say your name was?" he inquired, turning to André.

"André," he answered, mumbling it.

"Did you all hear that? André. Yes, André will do fine. Now, fellows, don't we have any better clothes for him?"

As easily and as quickly as that, André was absorbed into the organization. He was powerless to do anything one way or the other.

The more he became involved, the less he liked the look of things, but the less able he became to do anything. Gradually he was taken into the confidence of the gang. By a series of thinly-veiled threats, they let him know that it would not be easy to disentangle himself from this web, if he should ever be so inclined.

Little by little, André took on a whole new way of life. He was able to assimilate it almost as easily as he had put on the new clothes they gave him to replace his old rags.

Sometimes, at the beginning, André wondered whether he should ask the chief about that wallet he had picked up, and which he had never given back to André. But as he began to know what sort of a man the chief was, he realized that it was out of the question.

Nobody knew the chief's real name. He was referred to as the boss, the chief, or, when they were feeling a little insolent, 'the old man'. He was always spoken to politely to his face, and nothing he said could ever be contradicted. He treated any interruption while he was speaking as if it had not happened. Everybody was obliged to laugh at his 'jokes'. Needless to say, he did not live with the rest of the gang. Again, nobody knew where he lived.

Rumours about him were many and varied, and were sometimes aired, especially when the members of the gang were feeling insolent. They usually felt insolent on Saturday nights, when they had spent a good evening at the local bar.

There were ten men in the gang, mostly about André's age. They lived together in the large house to which André had been taken. A peculiar feature of their life was that each night one of them took turns to guard the house. This meant that one night in ten each of them went without sleep.

André was used at first on the smaller operations of the gang. He learnt the art of swindling people, getting money by trickery, and creating diversions for his accomplices who would carry out other things such as picking pockets. The irony did not escape André that it could well have been this gang which had robbed him that day at the port when all his money was stolen.

Very often they worked in the evenings, and sometimes at night. The only time they had off was on Saturday evenings, when they all went to the bar. At first, André could not bring himself to like the bar. The blaring music, the taste of the beer — all this was new to him, and he was glad when his turn came to stay at home on Saturday evening to guard the house.

In time, however, he became used to these things, and even looked forward to them. He became as eager as the rest of the gang to spend all his free time and money at the bar. He could not think how he had ever disliked the beer and the music.

Simon Returns to Mutondi

9 IT HAD BEEN A SAD DAY FOR Alphonse Mokunzu. He had watched the prize-giving and graduation ceremonies of the secondary school at Mutondi.

The same occasion last year filled his thoughts. He thought only of his son André, of how proud he had been of him, of how well he had done. He remembered also the last time he had seen his son, when he had been borne away from the village on the back of the truck.

Now it was many months since he had heard from André. He had written many times, by dictating the letters to his next son. Always the dictation was the same. What news of my son?

He had written to the last address André had given him, that of his brother, and he had written to the missionaries in Kinshasa, asking them what news they had of André, and asking if they could take special pains to try and find him. The replies he received were always the same — no news of André.

When he returned from the school ceremony, he went to his room and stayed there for an hour in prayer, pouring out his heart before his God.

When he emerged from his room, his wife was waiting for him. "You have been weeping, my husband," she said. "You have been yearning for André."

"Yes," he sighed. "I have vowed before the Lord to go and search for him."

She drew in her breath, then released all her emotions in a flood of tears. "Do you know how I have made it my daily prayer that God will bring André back to us?"

"No, I only know that my heart aches for André. Not knowing what has become of him, that is unbearable. I only know that I must go and search until I find him."

"How can we afford it?" she asked. "The crops have not been good this year."

"That is not the thing to think of. Our son is more important than anything else. If God wants me to go, then He will take care of our money."

They slept little that night. Their minds were full of thoughts of André and of his father's forthcoming journey.

The next day, they were up early, and Alphonse began making arrangements to get enough money, and for his journey and stay in Kinshasa.

He had just left the house when he heard the sound of running footsteps behind him, and a voice calling his name.

"Tata Mokunzu! Alphonse Mokunzu!"

The voice was familiar, and yet he could not

place it. He turned round to see who it was. He saw a young, smartly-clad figure. At once he knew who it was.

"Simon! You have returned! How can you come back to us after what you have done to us?"

"Oh, Tata, please forgive me. I know you have a right to be angry. Yes, I stole from you, and ran away with the money. But please listen to what I have to tell you." The words rushed out, with a childish impatience.

Alphonse remembered again what he had said to André before he left for Kinshasa. He had forbidden him to even think of revenge on Simon. He was immediately and bitterly sorry for his harsh words.

"I am sorry — yes, I forgave you a long time ago, but it was a shock to see you again suddenly after all this time."

"Yes, listen to what I have to say. Since I ran away to Kinshasa, I have become a Christian. So after my own family, you are the first person I have come to see since I returned."

Alphonse was overjoyed. "Come into the house and we will talk," he said.

His wife had by this time left the house, and they were alone.

Simon was the first to speak. "I have come to ask your forgiveness, but also there is another matter. Now that I am a Christian, I must right my wrongs. Look — I have come to repay the money I stole."

He held out an envelope. Alphonse stared unbelievingly, afraid to touch it.

"How can I take your money?" he gasped. "You must have paid for your mistake in many other ways."

"Yes, and heavily. But this is like a burden on my back. I can never rest until I have paid it back to you."

Alphonse made a sudden move towards the money, then took his hand back. He stood, staring, wondering, for a full minute.

"Please," said Simon, "you must take the money. My faith is weak. If I keep this money, I don't know what will happen to me. You must take it." He placed it firmly in Alphonse's hand.

"Truly, I can see how God has led us both. André, my oldest son went to Kinshasa a year ago, and now I have not heard from him for many months. I have decided to go and search for him, and now I know for sure that it is God who has led me to do this. For until now I did not know where I could get enough money to go and look for him."

"Then let me go," Simon cut in. "I know Kinshasa very well . . ."

"No, I must go myself, and find my son. This very morning when I saw you, I was on the way to make arrangements for the journey, and to find some money for it."

"Truly, God has been good to both of us, Tata Alphonse."

André Attempts to Escape

10 THINGS HAD BEEN QUIET FOR SOME weeks, and it was a welcome relief when one of the gang announced the arrival of the chief one evening.

He made a grand entrance, smiling condescendingly at the gang. "Leave me alone for a few minutes with Michel," he announced.

This event seemed to announce that something important was going on, for Michel was the second in command.

The others waited expectantly, and a buzz of excited conversation broke out. A few minutes passed, and they were all beckoned into the room again.

The chief and Michel sat at the table in the middle of the room. The buzz of conversation continued as the rest of the gang came in and found their places.

André was the first to see it, lying on the table, looking ugly in its starkness. One by one, the others noticed it, and the babble died down until there was an awed silence. Finally, the chief spoke.

"Well, now that you've all had a look at it, let's

talk business, eh?" Once again he laughed heartily. There were some half-hearted attempts to join in the laughter from the rest of the gang. André remained silent, for what he saw sent a chill down his spine.

"Where did you get it?" asked one of them.

The chief turned a fierce eye in the direction of the questioner. He stared long and menacingly at him.

"Any more questions?" he asked.

Silence.

He resumed his cheerful tone of voice. "Good, now we can talk seriously. You boys must remember that we don't want to stagnate. This," he picked up the gun as he said it, "will help us all to succeed in our work. You all want to get on in life, don't you? With this gun we can go on to bigger and better things. Now, I haven't much time, so listen carefully. I won't repeat myself. I don't want you all rushing to use it. Michel here," he put his other hand on the second in command's shoulder "will be in charge of the gun. He will also be answerable to me if any of you get into trouble with it."

André was not listening any more. He was in a cold sweat. His only idea was to escape as far as possible from this evil man and his group of criminals. André suspected that most of the others had been ensnared into this just as he himself had been. He saw himself being drawn further into the mesh, and he did not know where it would end. There was only one way to save himself. He would have to escape.

André did not remember anything else that happened that night. He did not remember how the chief left, or what he did later that evening. But that night he lay in bed working out his escape plan.

Escaping would not be easy. He had already received half-veiled threats of retribution if he ever tried to escape. Now that they had the gun, they would be even less likely to let anyone go who had incriminating evidence against them.

First of all, André decided, he would have to choose what few things he would take, and just leave the rest behind. He would spend as little of his money as he could, without it being noticeable, and save the rest to buy a ticket home.

He would have to buy his ticket in advance, and arrange that he would be on guard duty on the night before the boat left for home. Then he could slip away quietly in the night. He would be away before they noticed he was gone — that, at least, was how he tried to convince himself.

Of course, it may take a little time to arrange it for the proper night, but it would be worth waiting a little while if he could only make sure of getting away.

* * * * * * *

Alphonse Mokunzu trudged wearily up to the door. At last he had found the house. He raised his hand, and knocked apprehensively, calling at the same time.

In a moment, the door opened, and he saw the face of his brother. The face broke into a broad smile when its owner saw him.

For a moment, both stood silent.

Then, simultaneously:

"Pierre."

"Alphonse."

Their arms were clasping each other in the warm affection of two brothers who had not seen each other for years.

Alphonse was the first to break the silence. "It has been a long time. Truly it has lightened the burden of my soul to see you, my brother."

"You are troubled, Alphonse, yes. I can imagine your trouble with André."

"Yes, that is all that I can think about these days. Oh, if only I knew where he was."

"Oh, my brother," said Pierre, "I knew it would not finish well. I do not know where he is, and I have not seen him at all since he left me. I must be frank. He left here in anger, for he had been rude to us. Indeed, I must say that he had been very difficult."

"Oh, my son, my son!" wailed Alphonse.

Pierre ushered him into the house. He wanted to ease his brother's burden, so he said, "You may, of course, stay with us for as long as you need, my brother."

"Yes, Pierre, I will stay until I find him," said Alphonse.

*　*　*　*　*　*　*

All was ready. André had bought his ticket, and had put together all the things he would need — a small parcel. Now, he was preparing to go on guard duty for the night.

The night was refreshingly cool. A cloudless sky shone with a million tropical stars, and a bright full moon. André took his place on the little stool outside the door. He sat there quivering with excitement at the prospect of escape. In a little while, he got up and made his first tour, collecting pieces of wood for his fire, as was his custom.

Everything had to appear normal. André had to stay on duty half the night before he could make a move. No sense in spoiling everything now through over-anxiousness.

By the time he had done his fourth tour, the strain of waiting was beginning to tell on him. Usually it was difficult to keep awake, and the occasional getting up to walk round helped to keep him awake. Tonight, he could not have slept if he had tried.

At last, André decided it was time to make his move. The fire was stoked up well enough to last quite a long while.

He put his key into the door, and slowly turned it, then pushed the door gently. It creaked open with what seemed to André's tensed nerves like an ear-splitting crack. He remained still and silent for a full minute. Nothing happened!

He slowly tiptoed through the hall, and along the corridor. He reached his room. Slowly he turned the handle, the door opened silently, and André breathed a sigh of relief. So far so good.

He felt his way to the foot of his bed in the pitch black. He moved along the side of the bed on his hands and knees. The next obstacle would be to get his things from under the bed and the ticket from under the pillow without making any noise. He crept slowly and silently alongside the bed until he reached the place where he could stretch his arm under the bed, and . . .

His hand touched something which should not have been there. A foot.

The foot suddenly came into action. It lashed out in a vicious kick, which caught André on the shoulder. The force of it sent his crouching body reeling backwards. The wall hit him from behind with a sickening thud.

He lay there, half dazed, against the wall. Suddenly, with a click, everything was brightness. André put a weak and shaking hand up to his eyes. Against the light he could see a silhouetted figure.

His eyes slowly accustomed themselves to the light. He tried to straighten up a little. There was a dull ache where his shoulder should have been. He recognized the silhouette — Michel.

"Looking for something?" Michel said.

"What do you mean?" André stammered.

"Do you always keep a small bundle of clothes under your bed?" Michel's voice was quiet and mocking. "Or perhaps you forgot that yesterday you went to the river port and got this." With a flourish he produced the ticket for the boat.

"But — But . . ." was all that André could manage.

"My friend, the chief doesn't like people going without saying goodbye. Especially when we have this." He produced the gun from his pocket and waved it in André's direction.

André squirmed, trying to get out of the line of the gun.

"Quietly, my friend. We don't want to wake the others, do we?"

André's mind was working overtime, trying to find some way out.

"We wouldn't want anybody to know about this little, er, shall we say, lapse. Especially the chief. If the chief knew, he would be very angry. Do you know what the chief does when he is very angry? No, you don't of course. The chief was angry with one of the gang once before. You came along to replace that one, if you see what I mean."

André saw only too clearly what he meant. He still did not know where all this was leading to. He shifted his aching body, and went slowly to the bed, and stretched himself out.

"Are you comfortable? Good. Where was I? Ah, yes, I think it would be better for you if I didn't tell the chief what happened tonight. Don't you think so?"

André remained motionless.

"Yes, of course you agree. But you must realize that I am running a risk in not telling the chief. If he thought I was not keeping an eye on you lads . . ."

He drew a significant finger sharply across his throat.

André realized now what all this was leading to. He drew himself up on one elbow, and tried to sound as tough as he could.

"All right, how much do you want to keep quiet?"

"I knew you would see it my way. But there is no need for us to deal with all the sordid details now. I will take care of the financial side of things. All your money comes through me anyway. So let us just say that if I have any little extra needs, I needn't bother about asking you for it. No, that would be embarrassing to both of us. I can just keep it back before I give you your money."

"No!" said André, despairingly.

"Very well, we will forget the whole arrangement, and I will just tell the chief, and leave him to settle the matter." He turned as if to leave the room.

"All right," said André, "you win. I don't seem to have much choice, do I?"

"No, you don't, do you?" said Michel, as if the thought surprised him. He smiled, and left the room.

André watched him leave, and fell back on his bed. He was powerless and hopeless. Michel had a complete hold over him. All André could do was to watch Michel take as much money as he liked.

In his desperation, he lay on his bed, weeping silently to himself. He found himself thinking of his father again.

He also thought of his father's God, and his thoughts formed themselves into a prayer. "Oh, God, if there is a God, I've got myself into a complete mess. I can't get out of it. In fact I know I don't really deserve to get out of it. But if I ever do get out, I'll change, I promise I'll change." After this, he found his imagination running away with his thoughts. He was making all sorts of vows and promises that he never intended. Finally his thoughts came to rest, through lack of momentum. "What am I doing, making all these religious vows? I don't even know who I'm making them to. But one thing I know, if I do get out of this hell, I'll change. I've had enough of this life."

He was sinking slowly to sleep after the nervous and emotional strain, when a rough hand shook him awake. Michel again.

"Outside — guard duty. Remember, I'm watching, and I've got that ticket of yours," he snapped.

André passed the rest of the night uncomfortably and gloomily meditating on the hopelessness of his position. Michel had him where he wanted him. There was nothing he could do.

André is Reunited with his Father

11 IT WAS EVENING. A WEARY Alphonse Mokunzu returned to his brother's house after another fruitless day.

"My brother," said Pierre, "things do not go well for you. It is already a month you have been here. Every day you return unsuccessful."

"I have met a few people who have seen André."

"When?"

"Alas, they have not seen him for a long time. My son used to go to church with them. I have even met a man with whom he stayed for a few days, when he first arrived."

"Can they tell you nothing?" asked Pierre, anxiously.

"Nobody has seen him for months. But, oh! the rumours about him! I could die of the shame! Some say he is a beggar. Some say he is a gangster." Alphonse buried his head in his hands for a moment.

He looked up, and just caught the ghost of an expression of mockery on his brother's face.

The expression disappeared as Pierre spoke.

"Come," he said, in a superior manner. "You are tired, my brother. You must rest. But why go on torturing yourself this way? Why do you not return home? If André is found, I will personally see to it that he gets back to you safely. But if it is true what people say, I fear there is not much chance of ever . . ."

Alphonse looked at him unbelievingly, and broke in, angrily, "Do you really think that would cause me to abandon him?"

Pierre did not reply.

"Yes, I really do believe you would think that."

"But, my brother, I was suggesting nothing of the sort . . ."

"I know my son. I am a Christian. How could I possibly abandon him now? I don't believe even you would abandon one of your own children." Alphonse's voice was quickening. "No, there is no question, I must stay until I find him. I don't expect you to understand this, but I believe that God sent me here to find my son, and I believe God will help me to find him. And if you, my own brother, do not make me welcome, I will stay with others, who will help me."

With this outburst, he stalked out of the room. In his own room, he collapsed on his bed, and wept, and prayed. All he wanted was to see his boy, to find him, and to hold him.

*   *   *   *   *   *   *

The day started for André as any other day would start. He went through the routine of every morning, finishing with the meeting in the big room. Here, Michel, or sometimes the chief, would tell them what was going to happen during the day, and anything else they needed to know.

For some reason, this morning, André found himself thinking of the way his family used to start each day, back home in the village. He thought of how his father used to gather them all together for prayers before the day's work started. That village life of so long ago — would he ever see it again? The thought produced a kind of despair in him.

André pulled together his scattered thoughts, as he heard his name.

"Mokunzu — you are with us two today at the central market."

André knew what this meant. They were to mingle with the crowd, and pick up what they could from the pockets of the people, either in money or in objects of value. It was the most boring thing he could think of to do.

As was their custom, the three who were engaged in this activity would meet at a certain place at regular intervals, and if there was much in the way of valuables, one of them would take them to their receiver, to convert into cash.

The morning wore on, and André became tired and anxious to go home again. His now professional eye took in the people hurrying this way and that.

Suddenly, his heart skipped a beat. Surely he must be deluded — the heat must be playing tricks with his brain.

Even from behind, he would recognize that man anywhere. The man turned slowly, until André could see his profile. He could not believe that standing not five yards away from him was his own father.

His mind in a turmoil, he did not know what to do. He wanted to turn and run away, but he also wanted to run and embrace his father. He stood, frozen to the spot.

His father had turned, and saw his son. He also stood still for a moment, then rushed towards him, crying, "André, André."

André could not make his legs respond. Surely, he felt, he should be able to put some emotion into his face. Did he not feel happy to see his father? Why could he not smile? Why could he not cry? Every part of André seemed cold and paralysed.

Suddenly, he was engulfed in a firm embrace. Life came back to him, and he broke into choking sobs. He could no longer hold back the shame, but all he could say was, "Father, Father."

His father was similarly overcome. He said nothing, but clung tightly to his son, as if unwilling to relax his grip. He seemed to fear that something would take his son away again if he loosed his grip.

They did not know how long they remained like this. It could have been but a moment; it could have been hours. Slowly they disengaged themselves, parted, and looked at each other in silence. The silence seemed to engulf the noise and bustle around them. In that silent communion, more passed between them than any words could have said.

As for Alphonse, he saw his son no longer a child, as he had been when he left them. He read in his son's face all the anguish and misery he had been through. Somehow he knew that his son had slipped into a life of which he was ashamed, and that he wanted to escape from it.

André saw deep into his father's heart. He saw only love, and pity, and acceptance.

Alphonse spoke first. "André, my son, you are in trouble?" It was at once an affirmation as well as a question.

"Yes, Father," André replied, quietly, "but I am afraid that you cannot rescue me. I am trapped. You can only be happy that you have set eyes on me and leave."

"My son, that is enough of this silly talk. Nothing is hopeless. I believe that God has sent me to find you, and I cannot leave now without you."

"I cannot say anything more, please do not ask me, Father."

His father took his arm, and led him to a quieter street.

"Now," he said, firmly. "Tell me."

André hung his head and remained silent. Although he knew he was already forgiven, the shame of telling his father what he had become was too much.

"Look at me! Now tell me!" His father's voice was firm, yet so charged with emotion that he finally conveyed to his son that it really did not matter what he had done. He need not worry about telling his father.

Little by little, Alphonse got an outline of the whole story from André.

"And you are still with the gang, André?"

"Yes, Father, but it is useless. I cannot escape."

"But surely this would not be too difficult, my son."

"I have already tried, Father, and I tell you it is no good."

"You have tried to escape?" His father's voice had a new lightness in it. This was what he wanted to hear. He had known, instinctively, that this was not the sort of life his son would choose for himself. Hearing this, confirmed what he had known about his son.

"Yes, Father, I have tried, but I failed. They say that the only way to leave the gang is in a coffin . . ."

His words were interrupted by the sound of running footsteps. They turned towards the sound, and André's heart sank. It was Michel.

"André, what do you think you are doing?" shouted Michel.

André was at first seized with a desire to run. Yet he knew now that his place was with his father. Even if he had to die now, it seemed somehow worthwhile. Something like courage flooded through him. It was a strange, warm feeling. He had never felt it before.

André's father spoke to Michel. "I think you are mistaken. This is my son."

His voice was firm — even hard. It contained something which André in his world had not heard or recognized for a long time — a sort of uprightness. It challenged any kind of deviousness or crookedness.

Michel ignored the words, and spoke to André. His voice contained that veiled menace which he knew so well. "André, you must come. Whoever this is, you will make a great mistake if you do not come."

"Once again," cut in André's father, "I tell you that you are making a mistake. My son will not come with you."

André stood, helpless.

Michel appeared unsure of himself. Once again, André's father spoke.

"What are you, a thief or something?" He raised his voice, and some passers-by stopped and looked.

Just then, Michel panicked. Fear came into his face, and he turned and ran. The passers-by took up the cry of "Thief, thief!" and gave chase.

André stood rooted to the spot. His father's face

broke into a smile, and he chuckled to himself.

"I don't think we will see him for a while," he said.

Yes, thought André, but only for a while. "But what do we do now, Father? We can never escape."

"Don't lose hope, André. We will go now to stay with Pierre and then return home."

"But will Uncle Pierre take me in?"

"I am staying with Uncle Pierre, and he has agreed to take both of us for as long as we need to stay. Now, let us go."

To André's surprise they reached his uncle's house safely. He kept looking over his shoulder, expecting the gang to pounce on them at every turn.

The meeting with Uncle Pierre was strained. His uncle made a great show of forgiving André, but André could tell it was all an act. Finally he shook his uncle's hand, and was glad, at last, to be alone — really alone — with his father in their room.

A new wave of intimacy passed between them, as had not been possible before.

"Father, I really did want to return home. You do believe me, don't you?"

"Yes, of course, my son. I can see it in your face."

"I still want to get out of this hell of a mess, but it's like a net, and I'm too entangled in it. I just can't see it being as easy as you seem to think."

"That was strong language for a son of mine."

"Sorry, Father, I forgot."

"Don't worry — it does not shock me."

"But it really is like hell to me. I suppose you could say it's my own hell."

"André, you don't realize what that means. Have you forgotten all you used to read in the Bible?"

"Father, look I must tell you now. I never really did hold your beliefs. When I started to have doubts, which was even before I left home, you never encouraged me to talk about them. So I remained silent. Once I arrived here, it didn't seem to matter any more whether I believed or not. Nothing I could remember about the Bible, or Christianity had anything at all to do with life here."

André's father sat in silence for a moment, then went to his bed. From under the pillow he brought out his Bible. Slowly he searched through it until he found what he was looking for.

André sat watching. He was sad that what he had just said brought bitterness to his father. Yet it was better that his father should know the truth.

"I cannot convince you of anything, André. But just read from Luke's gospel, somewhere near the middle of chapter fifteen. Start reading where it is written: 'A certain man had two sons'."

"But father . . ."

"Just read it, please, André. Like you used to

do at home."

André sighed. "Here it is. 'A certain man had two sons. The younger of them said to his father, "Father, give me my share of the property." So the father divided the property between them.' "

André paused. "But I know this already, Father. I've read the story many times." He put the Bible on the bed.

"Never mind — just read it — for me."

"All right Father. Now, yes." He picked up the Bible again. " 'Not many days later, the younger son gathered all his belongings, and went on a journey to a place far away. There, he wasted all he had in loose living . . .' Really, Father, if this is pointed at me . . . Don't you know I'm sorry for the life I've led? Can't you see I'm sorry?"

"André, please calm down. I meant nothing of the sort. You should know by now how I feel about you."

"I am sorry, Father. It is not good for any son to speak to his father like that, least of all me to you."

"That's all right, André. I know that you are upset, but please carry on reading. I want to hear the rest of the story."

" 'When all his possessions had been used up, a great famine came upon that land, and he began to be in want. He went and became involved with one of the citizens of that country, and this man sent him into the fields to feed the pigs. He was so hungry that he even wanted to fill his stomach with the pods that the pigs ate, and nobody gave him anything.' "

André paused, and smiled inwardly. These familiar words were appropriate enough. His eyes skimmed the next sentences and he felt again that the words applied to him. He felt one up on the son in the story, however, for he had been in advance in his thoughts of returning home.

His father shot a questioning glance at him. He continued. " 'He thought in his heart, and said, "My father's hired workers have more than enough bread, but I am dying of hunger here. I will leave and go to my father. I will say to him, 'Father, I have done evil against heaven and in your eyes. I am not worthy to be called your son any more. Make me like one of your hired workers.'

" 'He left, and made his way back to his father. But while he was still a long way off, his father saw him, felt pity for him, and went running to him. He fell on his neck, and kissed him.' "

André's father's head sank to his chest as he heard these words. André saw that he was fighting hard to keep back his emotions.

André wanted to finish there, but his father looked up and beckoned him to read on.

" 'His son, however, said, "Father, I have done evil against heaven, and in your eyes. I am not worthy to be called your son." '

" 'But his father said to the servants, "Bring the finest clothes, quickly, and put them on him. Put a

ring on his finger and shoes on his feet. Bring the
fattened calf, and kill it. Let us eat and be glad.
This son of mine was dead, and is alive again; he
was lost, and is found . . ." '."

André's father could restrain himself no longer.
He embraced his son. The Bible fell to the ground,
and André tried to escape his father's embrace by
picking it up. His father held tight, and wept.

"Don't you see?" he cried through his tears,
"Don't you know how I felt when I first saw you?"

In a flash, André understood. He anticipated
what his father went on to say.

"It was as if you were dead, and had come alive
again. I am happy — no, I am more than that —
because you were lost, and now you are found.
Now that I've found you, I'm not going to lose you
again."

"But Father," André protested, "I am not worth
all this effort by you. Why should you search me
out when it was I who left you?"

"My son, my son. You must know that it is
because I love you. How can a father forget his
son? How can he exist without knowing what has
become of his son? Besides, I somehow knew
before I left the village that you were in trouble of
some kind. Knowing that, I also knew that you
would try to get back if you could."

"Father, at one point, I almost enjoyed the life
with the gang. I was nearly ready to give up any
thought of home. I am ashamed to admit it, but it

is true. You nearly lost me for good."

They said nothing more that evening. André's father slept more soundly than he had done for many a month.

André could not sleep. The reason was partly the emotional upheaval of finding out what he really wanted after all; but mostly for fear of what lay ahead. He looked and felt a nervous and physical wreck when his father woke up next morning.

He confessed his fears to his father.

"Don't worry, André. I believe that the Lord is in control."

"Well, what do we do now?" André asked.

"First of all, we are going to pray, André."

"But . . ." André started to interrupt, then thought better of it. He was anxious not to displease his father.

"Yes, I know André, you are not sure about praying."

"Well, Father . . ."

"Do not try to hide it for my sake, André. You have said to me already that you doubted. Yes, and let there be no question. That does not matter. I still love you. Remember that always, André. Whatever you do, or think, there could never be any conditions on a father's love."

"Do not go on like this," André said, hanging his head. "The shame is too much."

His father lifted up André's head. "There is just

one more thing I must say, André, and then I am finished. The story you read last night was a parable. Jesus told it to tell people what God is like. Now, although I got you to read the story last night because it showed what I felt, can you not also see yourself in that story. Have you wandered far from God? Then do not worry about Him accepting you, if you turn back to Him."

"I do not know what to think about that, Father," replied André, honestly. "I will say this — that I am more ready to think about it than I have ever been before. One thing I do know, though, is that we must do something quickly if we want to get out of here alive."

12

ANDRÉ'S FATHER BOWED HIS HEAD, and prayed. As always, it was a fervent prayer. André also bowed his head, but did not close his eyes, and only half-listened. His mind was too occupied with trying to think of some clever scheme. He just heard when his father's tone of voice changed.

". . . And Lord, finally, give us courage to make whatever sacrifice may be necessary. When the time comes to be brave, may we not fail you. Amen."

That day, André stayed at home, while his father went to the river port to buy the tickets.

"I have the tickets!" his father told him when he arrived home. "Come, André, take a pen and paper, and write to tell your mother when she may expect us home."

André obeyed, and wrote as his father dictated. He thought of his mother, and how good it would be to get home again, if they could make it.

When the letter was finished, his father went out to post it. They still had three days to wait before the departure of the boat, and André tried to impress on his father the necessity of staying in the house all the time, so as not to be seen by any of the gang.

"Father, I don't think you realize how dangerous this is going to be. I know how ruthless the gang is. The chief, that's what we call the leader . . ." he stopped, and repeated, in a shamefaced way, "that's what *they* call him, anyway. He's a cruel man, who lets nothing stand in his way. I know them well enough to know that they won't stand idle while a member of the gang is running loose knowing all about them — especially since they have a gun."

There was a pause, before his father spoke.

"Thank you for telling me this, André. But I must tell you that I know that the Lord hasn't forgotten us. I feel sure that the Lord intends you to get home safely. It's as if He had visited me personally, in this room, and given me His promise. I can't explain it any other way — I just know. That's all I can say. Can you understand that, André?"

"Yes, I think so, Father. But just promise me you won't go out of this house until we leave for the boat."

"I will promise you that I will not go out any more than I have to. However, there is at least one visit I must make. I must visit Ernest. You remember your first 'Uncle' in Kinshasa?"

"Oh, yes, but why do you have to see him? Just

tell me what you want to say and I will write a letter to him from you."

"No, André. He helped me very much. You yourself know better than I how much help he gave you. God would not be pleased if I were impolite to him. I must go to say farewell to him, and to tell him that I have found you. He has been praying for you ever since you left him."

"Then if you must go, give him my thanks. I did not reward him well by the way I lived, but that will change now. And please, Father, when you go to see him, be careful."

"Yes, André. I will be careful."

André was silent for a while, then he said, "Father, I feel so bad about what I have done, that I would hate anything to happen to you. It would make me feel terrible, because it would be my fault. You know, it's something like that with God. I feel too far gone for Him to forgive me. It may be all right for others, but I must be a hopeless case."

"No, son. Nobody is beyond God's love."

"Oh, it's not so much that. It's the way I've left God. Leaving home, looking for a job, these were all just steps away from God, as well as from you, Father. I just feel that I turned my back on Him, and that's an awful lot to forgive."

"But I love you, André, and I have forgiven you. Why shouldn't God do that?"

"It just seems as if it can't be that easy. Surely I must have to do something to make up for it?

What I mean is that I know very well that nobody gets anything for nothing. At least, I know that if I *do* get something for nothing, I don't value it. Everybody knows that."

"But, son, you didn't have to do anything for me to forgive you."

"No, but at least you knew that I wanted to come home and I tried."

"Then is it not the same with God?"

"I just don't know, Father."

"You must talk to the pastor when you get home, André. He will help you with this."

"I know that I just shan't feel it's real unless I can do something to make it up with God."

"I really don't know how to answer you, André. Just promise me you will speak to the pastor."

"Yes, Father. Let us go to sleep now. I am tired."

"So am I. I will pray now, for both of us."

André's father was tired, and he prayed more briefly than usual. He finished by saying the Lord's prayer, hoping that André would join in.

". . . And forgive us our trespasses, as we forgive those who sin against us . . ."

"That's it!" André exclaimed, interrupting his father's prayer.

"That's what, André?"

"Father, I have realized what is coming between myself and God."

"Tell me what it is, my son."

"What you said just now: 'Forgive us our trespasses as we forgive those that sin against us.' Don't you see, I have never felt that I should forgive anybody who did evil against me. Now, if I could forgive somebody, would that be enough for God? Would He be able to forgive me then?"

"But André . . ."

"And I know just the person I must forgive. Simon. Ever since he stole that money from us, I have never forgiven him. When I came to Kinshasa, I was on the look out for him all the time, and now if I forgive him . . . But is it enough to forgive somebody in your heart, Father? We shall never see him again."

"Oh, André, I had completely forgotten, in all the excitement of finding you." The words burst from his father. "Now, listen, and I will tell you something which I think will please you. Truly God has been good . . ." With this, he told André the whole story of how Simon had returned, and provided the means for him to come and search for André, by returning the stolen money.

André was silent. At first he felt resentment that Simon had taken away his chance to be magnanimous. Then he felt that perhaps, after all, he had not really forgiven Simon in his heart. This really was not how he had wanted it to happen. Perhaps after all, it would not be easy to get God's forgiveness. Then he voiced his feelings.

"I don't know at all, Father. I reckon that I'm

just not good enough yet."

"But André, you don't have to feel good to be forgiven."

"That's something I've heard a hundred times before. Yet I just don't know what to think, Father. Let us sleep now. My mind is tired from much thinking."

The next day, André's father went to see Ernest. To André's surprise, he returned safely, and did not think he had been followed.

"Ernest sends his greetings, André," he said. "He wishes us a safe journey, and he will be praying for us all the time."

"I only hope the journey is safe — though I very much doubt it."

"Ernest says he will also pray for you, that you might find what you are looking for — the assurance of forgiveness. He really is concerned for you. In fact," his father lowered his voice, "he cares for you as a real uncle should."

The next day dragged by, as if unwilling to meet the day of departure. Neither André nor his father ventured out of the house. At last, the great day dawned. The day of André's return.

Although he had anticipated this day for months, now that it had arrived, he seemed strangely ill at ease, and pessimistic.

"Father," he said, "we must be extra careful. I'm sorry to say this again, but I know how thorough the gang are. They are sure to know that the boat is leaving today, and if they are as careful as I think they are, they will be at the port."

"André, I have already said that we will be careful, and also that I believe that God is taking care of us. Do not fret."

"Well, the least we can do is to take a taxi to the port."

"Very well, son."

His father went out to call a taxi. After a cool and brief farewell to Uncle Pierre, they were on their way to the port.

As they approached, André told the driver to slow down and be ready for anything. To the driver, this was something a little different to normal, with a hint of adventure. He readily complied.

His father took the two tickets from his pocket, and gave one to André.

"If we are separated, board the boat alone," he said.

As they turned into the wide forecourt of the port, André crouched down on the floor of the taxi, so that he was not visible from the outside.

"Now, Father, keep on the look out. There is only one who would recognize you."

The taxi edged its way forward amongst the crowd. Suddenly, André's father exclaimed: "He's there! The one I saw with you."

The taxi made its way slowly forward until it reached the port entrance.

"Do we take a chance and enter now?" asked André.

"Just a minute," said his father, "I think one of them has seen me — yes, it's the one who saw us together."

"Oh, no," exclaimed André.

"Quick, driver," shouted his father, "turn round and leave as fast as you can."

The taxi executed a painfully slow turn amongst the crowd, and finally made its way out of the port.

"They've got another car, and they're coming after us," said André's father, as they started accelerating away from the port.

André sat up, and peered anxiously out of the back window.

"It's that red car," his father explained.

"Can you see it?" André asked the taxi-driver.

The driver nodded.

"Try and lose it," said André's father.

The driver accelerated even more as he turned a corner. He executed a series of sharp turns, in quick succession.

André and his father kept looking out of the back window.

Finally, André said, "Well, I think we've lost them."

The driver, feeling that it was himself who had lost them, said, "Now what?"

"Go back to the port, as fast as you can," instructed André's father. "We might slip in behind their backs."

The driver turned to head back to the port. He had gone only a few blocks when André, still looking out of the window, announced that he saw the red car behind them again.

"Have they seen us?" asked the driver.

"It looks like it," replied André.

"You'll have to lose them all over again," said André's father.

Once again, the driver accelerated, and swerved round corners, in another bid to lose their pursuers. Somehow, they never managed to shake them off this time, although the driver managed to keep a good distance between them.

Suddenly, André's father took two notes from his pocket, and said to the driver: "Round this next corner slow down, and we will get out and hide. You carry on, and lead them as far away as you can, without losing them." He pressed the two notes into the driver's pocket.

The driver slowed suddenly as they turned the corner. André's father leaned across André and opened the door. He had to push André out. He threw the suitcase out of the door, and finally jumped out himself.

André was dazed by the suddenness of his father's action. He was even more dazed by being sent sprawling in the road. He picked himself up, to hear and see the taxi speeding off down the road. He looked around, and went weak at the knees at what he saw. His father was wandering aimlessly in the road.

Their pursuers must be only seconds away. Then they would turn the corner, and . . .

13

André gathered his wits together. If he did nothing now, they were both lost. More likely, they would both be dead.

He rushed over to his father, and slapped his face.

"Come on Father!" he shouted.

He glanced up and down the street, and saw, a few yards away, a walled off garden. That would have to do. He guided his father towards the garden. At that moment he knew he must hear the car rounding the corner. He moved faster, dragging his father along by the arm. A final rush and they were there.

He pushed his father down, and flopped down beside him with the exhaustion of the effort. Just at that moment, the car screeched round the corner, and raced up the road.

André held his breath. The sound of the car grew fainter, and finally died away as it turned the corner. André still waited breathless, not daring to move. He waited a full minute. When all was still quiet, he got up, went into the street, and looked up and down. Still deserted.

But there, several yards away, was the suitcase André's father had thrown out, lying only half-hidden from the road by a parked car. Had they seen it? He decided that there was nothing he could do now, even if they had. He went to collect the case, and came back to his father, who was now sitting upright, looking around him.

He blinked and said, "What happened?"

"You were dazed, Father."

"Oh, my head." He put his hand up to a small cut on his forehead. He winced with pain. "My wrist as well. I think I've sprained it." Then, suddenly remembering what had happened, "Did the trick work?"

"Yes, Father. They're chasing the taxi now — at least I hope they are."

"We'd better get back to the port as quickly as we can."

He scrambled to his feet.

"No, you must rest," protested André.

"I'll be all right," his father protested. "Just let me lean on you, and we'll take it slowly."

After a half-hearted protest, André got up, and helped his father to his feet. Then he picked up the suitcase again. They made slow progress, and took half an hour to reach the port approach road, where André stopped and put down the suitcase.

"Now, Father," he said, "if they have been clever, as I guess they have, they will have left somebody at the port in case we go back. You wait here while I look and see if the way is clear."

His father agreed, and, with the suitcase, stood by the roadside trying to look inconspicuous. André advanced slowly, looking round all the time. He reached the end of the port approach road, and turned into the large courtyard in front of the port. So far, so good.

He edged his way along one side of the courtyard, still casting furtive glances all around. He reached the port entrance. Still nothing.

He ventured in, and looked slowly around the spacious hall. Everything was so normal it seemed almost eerie. André had the feeling he was entering a trap which would suddenly spring shut.

He waited several minutes in the main hall, and still saw no sign of any gang member. He decided that now was the time to take his courage in both hands, and bring his father back. He walked, again slowly and cautiously, back through the courtyard, and turned the corner up the port approach road.

André's father had been waiting patiently. He was watching every face to see if he recognized anybody.

The minutes ticked by, and still André did not return. He began to wonder what could have happened, and was on the point of going down himself. Suddenly, his blood froze.

A red car flashed by. He involuntarily crouched down so as not to be seen. The car was already yards past him, when he looked up, and recognized the occupants. It was their pursuers.

André was still down there, and something had to be done. He picked up the case and walked as quickly as he could towards the port.

A few seconds later, he noticed André turn from the port. He was walking unhurriedly, and had not seen his father coming towards him on the opposite side of the road.

Alphonse tried to walk faster towards André, but already his head was thumping with the effort. They were still about fifty yards apart when the red car turned from the port, and started slowly up the port approach road behind André.

They must have seen André, he thought. Suddenly he saw Michel, seated next to the driver, take something from inside his jacket.

Despite the pain in his head and wrist, and the weariness in his limbs he increased his speed. The car was drawing close to André. He saw now that Michel was pointing his arm towards André, and that in his hand was a gun . . .

Any second now, they would draw level with André. His reflexes took over from his mind, and the run became a sprint. He was now only yards from André, and the car rapidly closing in from behind. He ran desperately towards André, across the road, shouting, "André, look out!" With a final despairing effort, he flung the suitcase at the red car.

In his desperation, he had run into the road,

directly in front of a car going in the opposite direction to the red car. It swerved to avoid him, but only partially succeeded. It caught him a glancing blow, and again sent him sprawling in the road.

The suitcase was not so well aimed, and went hurtling towards the red car. The driver of this car had heard the shout, and looked that way in surprise. The window at his side being open, he saw the suitcase about to hit him, threw up his arms to protect himself, and lost control.

The car swerved, and collided head on with the car that had tried to avoid André's father. The two cars met with a squeal of brakes, a crunch of metal, and a splintering of glass.

There was a momentary hush, then a hubbub of commotion. A milling crowd collected around the accident. André was stunned when he saw his father dash across the road, and fall headlong as the car hit him from behind. His only concern now was for his father. He dashed round the crowd, to the other side of the main accident. His father, lying further away, was relatively unattended. André easily pushed his way through to him.

For the second time within an hour, his father was lying unconscious. André knelt down, and cradled his father's head in his arms. The original cut had opened up again, and there was now a fresh wound. He put his face close to his father's.

"Thank God," he whispered, "he's still alive."

He looked up appealingly at a man standing near to him.

"Will you help me carry my father to the port?" he asked.

The man nodded, and together they carried his father into the main hall of the port. An official saw them, and motioned them into an office. Already people were clearing desks and chairs out of the office.

They took his father in, and laid him on the floor.

"They'll need all this floor space," said the other man, "There are many more injured and dead."

André sat on the floor beside his father. He was still numbed. A few minutes later, another body was brought in, which he recognized as Michel. He looked questioningly at the man who had brought him in.

"Dead," said the man, simply.

André did not know whether he was glad or sorry. Soon, others were brought in; three more gang members — one of them dead — and the driver of the other car who was dead.

There were six bodies lying on the floor. The bearers waited. Other people came in and looked. The room was soon full. Then the port official entered, followed by another man.

"This," explained the official, "is a doctor. He is a passenger on the boat."

"Everybody must leave the room while I examine these people," ordered the doctor.

The official hustled all the people to the door. Finally, he came to André.

"Out!" he snapped. "You heard what the doctor said."

"But this is my father," André pleaded. He looked at the doctor.

"Let him stay," said the doctor, in a tired way.

André stood by while the doctor examined all six bodies. Finally, the doctor stood up.

"Three dead, three alive," he stated, baldly. Then, to the port official, "Do you have any bandages or medicines?"

"A few," he answered.

"Take me to them." He turned to follow him out of the room. Then he turned back to talk to André.

"Your father will live," he said. "He has quite a bad concussion, but the others are worse off. Now, if any of them move, don't touch them until I come back."

They left André alone in the closed room, with the six inert forms. All was suddenly silent. As the numbness wore off, the enormity of what had happened dawned upon him.

Three men were dead — one of them completely unconnected with him. The others were injured, and who knew what would happen to them?

Worst of all, his father, his own father had risked

his life to save him. If anything serious happened to his father, he would never forgive himself.

All this had happened because of him. André could not even question any more whether all this self-torture was wrong. In the nervous exhaustion of the moment, he put his head in his hands and wept.

He was still sobbing when the doctor returned.

The doctor paused as he entered, and went to André.

"I told you your father was all right," he said. "He will have to go to hospital with the rest when the ambulance comes, but . . ."

André looked up, alarmed:

"But we have tickets for the boat. We must go home, especially now that . . ." He stopped himself.

"You're in trouble of some kind, aren't you?" said the doctor, and continued, without waiting for an answer, "It's a good job for you that I am also a passenger on the boat. How far are you going?"

"Five day's journey, sir."

"Good, I'm going further than that myself. I will arrange for you to travel with your father under my care."

With that, he bent down to tend the wounds of the three injured men. He did so in silence, while André stood by awkwardly. As the doctor finished, the port official returned.

The doctor rose up slowly, and asked André for his tickets. "These two are travelling under my care," he pronounced, handing over the two tickets. "Have you telephoned for the ambulance yet?"

"Yes, it will come soon."

"Please get these two on board, and I will wait with the others until the ambulance arrives." The doctor gave it as an order.

The port official helped André carry his father to the boat, and found their cabin. Finally, André and the official lowered his father into the bed.

André sat down beside the bed, and waited. Exhaustion overwhelmed him. Gradually his head sunk lower until it came to rest on the bed, beside his father.

Suddenly, he felt a movement. He looked up. A long time must have elapsed, for it was now dark. But what had moved?

His father still lay unmoving on the bed. He looked around, and through the window. The boat was moving! The port lights were drifting past his window, and getting farther away. Was it a dream? Could they really be safe at last? He heaved a great sigh of relief, as he realized that he was not dreaming.

Several minutes later, his father stirred.

"Father," said André, "we're really on our way. We're going home at last."

"At last," sighed his father, and smiled a contented smile, as his head sank back on the pillow.